t 199
.45

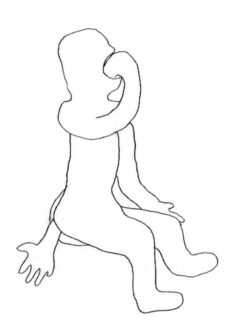

ELECTRIC

no.3
WINTER 2010

COVER

Trimspa
oil on board 48" x 56"
Adam Cvijanovic

INSIDE DRAWINGS
Adam Thompson

ELECTRIC LITERATURE NO.3

Andy Hunter ···{ *Co-publisher, Editor-in-Chief*

Scott Lindenbaum ···{ *Co-publisher, Editor*

Jeff Price ···{ *Associate Editor*

Molly Auerbach, Anna Prushinskaya,
Christopher Scotton, Benjamin Samuel ···{ *Editorial Assistants*

Bill Smith, designsimple.com ···{ *Designer*

Katie Byrum ···{ *Copy Editor*

Readers
Lois Bassen, Henry Chapman, Sarah Codraro, Dan Coxon, Heidi Diehl,
Noia Efrat, Nora Fussner, Rafi Ginsburg, Erin Harte, JT Hill, Addie Hopes,
Brian Hurley, Jessica Jacobs, Andy Kelly, Susan Kendzulak, Jennifer Kikoler,
Sharon Knauer, Travis Kurowski, James Langlois, Kate Petty, Chloe Plaunt,
Christine Rath, Kirsten Rohstedt, Helen Rubinstein, Richard Santos,
Evelyn Spence, Liz Stevens, Michael Stutz, Raina Washington,
Anna Wiener, Christopher Yen

Special Thanks
Kendra Atkin, Jonathan Ashley, Jordan Holberg, Richard Nash, Donna K.,
Alice Cohen, Robert Cohen, Myles David Jewell, Peggy and Richard Price,
Alison Elizabeth Taylor, Brian Lindenbaum, Bruce Lindenbaum,
Barry Roseman, Alan Roseman, Jim Shepard, Larry Benowich, Ben George,
Catherine Bohne, Helen Phillips, Kyle Semmel, Matthew Korahais,
Lucky Lee, Bulldog Gin, David Hirmes

For subscriptions, submission information, or to advertise,
visit our website at **electricliterature.com**

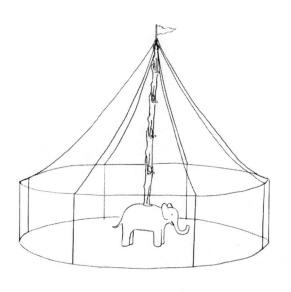

EDITORS' NOTE

We often hear that no one reads anymore, and yet everywhere we look, we see people reading—whether it be books, blogs, tweets, SMS-messages, or editors' notes. So before we write the epitaph for the literary age, we thought, *let's try it this way first*: select stories with a strong voice that capture our readers and lead them somewhere exciting, unexpected, and meaningful. Be entertaining without sacrificing depth. Make it streamlined—just five great stories an issue. And publish in every viable medium: paperback, Kindle, iPhone, audiobook, and eBook.

Electric Literature's greater mission is to use new media and innovative distribution to keep literature a vital part of popular culture. We were the first literary magazine to publish on the iPhone and the first to launch a YouTube channel. Rick Moody's "Some Contemporary Characters", appearing in this issue, was first published on Twitter.com as a three-day experiment in micro-serialization.

New media allows publishers, writers, and readers to connect in new ways. We continue to brainstorm on the opportunities for storytelling that new technology presents. Visit our website, join our Facebook page, follow us on Twitter (@ElectricLit), and sign up for our email list to stay updated on what's coming next.

At the heart of all this is our love of stories. We hope you enjoy the five in this issue.

Sincerely,
Andy Hunter & Scott Lindenbaum
Editors

electricliterature.com
editors@electricliterature.com

Contents

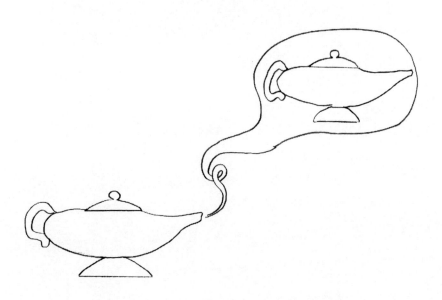

The Red Ribbon

It began with his fantasy, told to her one night over dinner and wine at l'Oiseau d'Or, a French restaurant with tiny gold birds etched into every plate and bowl.

"My college roommates," he said, during the entrée. "Once brought home."

"Drugs?"

"Women," said Daniel softly, "that they paid for." Even in candle-light, she could track the rise of his blush.

"Prostitutes?" Janet said. "Is that what you mean? They did?"

The kitchen doors swung open as the waiter brought a feathery dessert to the table next to theirs.

"I did not join in, Janet," Daniel said, reaching over to clasp her hand tightly. "Never. Not once. But I sometimes think about the idea of it. Not really it, itself—"

"The idea of it."

"I never once joined in," Daniel repeated.

"I believe you," said Janet, crossing her legs. She wondered what the handsome couple sharing the chocolate mousse would make of this con-versation, even though they were laughing closely with each other and seemed to have no need for anyone else in the restaurant. She herself had noticed everyone else in the restaurant while waiting for the pâté to ar-rive, dressed in its sprig of parsley: the older couple, the lanky waiter, the women wrapped in patterned scarves. Now she felt like propelling herself into one of their conversations.

"I'm upsetting you," he said, swirling fork lines into his white sauce.

"Not so much," she said.

Aimee Bender   19

"Nevermind," he said. "Really. You look so beautiful tonight, Janet."

On the drive home, she sat in the backseat, as she did on occasion. He said it was to protect her from more dangerous car accidents; she liked thinking for a moment that he was her chauffeur, that she had reached a state of adult richness where you did nothing for yourself anymore and returned to infancy. She imagined she had a cook, a hairdresser, a bath-filler. A woman who came over to fluff her pillow and tuck her in. Daniel turned on the classical music station and a cello concerto spilled out from the speakers in the back, and from the angle of her seat, Janet could just catch a glimpse of the bottom of her nose and top of her lips in the rear view mirror. She stared at them for the entire ride home. Her nose had fine small bones at the tip, and her lipstick, even after dinner, was unsmudged. There was something deeply soothing to her in this image, in the simplicity of her vanity. She liked how her upper lip fit inside her lower lip, and she liked the distance between the bottom of her nose and the top of her mouth. She liked the curve of her ear. And in those likings and their basic balance, she felt herself steady, as Daniel drove.

‹› ‹› ‹›

Back at home, she spent longer than usual in the bathroom, suddenly rediscovering all the lotion bottles in the cabinet that were custom-made for different parts of the body. For feet, for elbows, for eyes, for the throat. Like different kinds of soil that need to be tilled with different tools. When she entered the bedroom, fully cultivated, skin stenciled by a lace nightgown, the lights were off. Only the moon through the window revealed the tiny triangles of skin beneath the needlework.

"Time for bed, honey," she said cheerily, which was code that meant don't touch me. But there was no real need; his back already radiated the grainy warmth of sleeping skin. She slid herself between the sheets and called up another picture, this one of Daniel, a green bill wrapped around his erection like a condom. The itch of the corners of the bill as they pricked inside her. His stuff all over the faces of presidents. Stop it now Janet, she thought to herself, but she finally had to take a pill to get the image out of her head; it made her too jittery to sleep.

Daniel went to work at the shoe store in the morning, suit plus vest, and Janet slept in, as usual. Her afternoons were wide open. Today, after she had wrested all the hot water out of the shower, she went straight to a lingerie shop to buy a black bustier. She remained in the dressing room for over twenty minutes, staring at her torso shoveled into the satin.

"So, Janet," called the saleslady, Tina, younger and suppler, "is it lovely? Does it fit?"

Janet pulled her sweater on and went up to the counter.

"It fit," she said, "and I'm wearing it home. How much?"

Tina, now at the cash register, snapped a garter belt between her fingers. "I need the little tag," she said, "this isn't like a shoe store."

Janet inhaled to full height, had some trouble breathing out because her ribs were smashed together, and said, sharply: "Give me the price, Tina. I will not remove this piece of clothing now that it's on, so I either pay for it this way or walk out the door with it on for free."

When she left the store, receipt tucked into her purse, folded twice, emboldened, Janet thought of all the chicken dishes she had not sent back even though they were either half-raw or not what she had ordered. Chicken Kiev instead of Chicken Marsala, Chicken with Mushrooms instead of Chicken à la king: her body was made up of the wrong chickens. She remembered Daniel's first insistent kiss by the bridge near the Greek café on that Saturday afternoon. She hadn't thought of it in years and she could almost smell the schwarma rotating on its pole outside. He had asked her out again, and again, and told her he loved her on the fourth date, and bought her fancy cards inside of which he wrote long messages about her smile.

By seven o'clock that night, all the shoes in Daniel's shoe store were either sold or back in boxes and clip clop clip came his own up the walkway. The sky was dimming from dark blue into black and Janet sat in the brightly lit hallway, legs crossed, bustier pressing her breasts out like beach balls, the little hooks fastened one notch off in the back so that she seemed a bit crooked.

Daniel paused in the doorway with his briefcase. "Oh my," he said, "what's this?"

She felt her upper lip twitching. "Hello, Daniel," she said, "welcome home."

She stood awkwardly and approached him. She tried to remember: Be slow. Don't rush. Removing his coat and vest and laying them evenly on the floor, she reached into the back of his pants and pulled out his walnut-colored wallet. He watched, eyes huge, as she sifted through the bills until she found what she wanted. That handsome Mr. Franklin.

He usually used the hundred dollar bill to buy his best friend Edward from business school a fine lunch with fine wine on their sports day.

She waved it in his face.

"Okay?" she said.

He grabbed her waist as she tucked the bill inside the satin between her breasts.

"Janet?" he said.

She pushed him onto the carpet and began to take off the rest of his clothes. Halfway through the buttons on his shirt, right at his ribs, she was filled with an enormous terror and had to stop to catch her breath.

"For a week, Daniel," she whispered, trembling, "each time. Okay? Promise?"

His breathing was sharp and tight. "A week," he said, adding figures fast in his head, "of course, I would love a week, a week," and his words floated into murmur as she drove her body into his.

They forgot about dinner. They stayed at that spot on the carpet for hours and then tumbled off to the bedroom, his coat and vest resting flat on the carpet. He stroked the curve of her neck with the light brown mole. She fell asleep first.

«» «» «»

On Wednesday, Janet heard Daniel call Edward and cancel their lunch date. "I'm just too busy this week," he'd said; Janet smiled to herself in the bathtub. He brought her handfuls of daffodils. "My wife doesn't love me," he told her in bed, which made her laugh from the deep bottom of her throat. She put a flower between her teeth and danced for him, naked, singing too loud. He grabbed her and pushed her into chairs and she kept singing, as loud as she possibly could, straddling him, wiggling, until finally he clamped a hand over her mouth and she bit his palm and slapped his thighs until they flushed pink. When it was over she felt she'd shared something fearfully intimate with him and could barely look him in the eye, but he just handed her the hundred and went into the bathroom.

On their wedding day, Daniel had given her a card with a photograph of a beach on it. "You are my fantasy woman," he'd written inside. "You come to me from my dreams." It had annoyed her then, like a bug on her arm. I come to you from Michigan, she had told him. From 928 Washington Street. He'd laughed. "That's what I love so much about you, Janet," he'd said, whirling her onto the dance floor. "You're no-nonsense," he said. She spent the song trying furtively to imitate Edward's wife, who danced like she had the instruments buzzing inside her hips.

«» «» «»

By the end of the week, 900 dollars nestled in her underwear drawer. She put the bills on the ironing board and flattened them out, faces up, until they were so crisp they could be in a salad.

She'd thought about buying a dress. My whore dress! she'd thought. She'd considered ninety lipsticks. My hooker lips! she'd thought. Finally she just tucked the cash into her purse and took herself to lunch. Thirty dollars brought her to the best bistro in the area, where she had a hamburger and a glass of wine. The juice dripped down, red-brown, and left a stain on her wrist.

"Ah, fuck you," she said to the homeless man on the street who asked for change. "You really think I can spare any of my NINE HUNDRED DOLLARS that I made by SELLING MY BODY?"

The man shook his head to the ground. "Sorry ma'am," he said. "I never would have guessed."

"And don't you GOD BLESS ME," she yelled at the man, from down the block.

"I will not," he called back. "I have no interest in blessing you at all."

Once she was home she couldn't stand to sit down. She couldn't move or answer the phone. Breathing felt like an enormous burden.

She took an hour getting dressed in a pressed navy blue suit she'd never worn before but had bought because it was on sale and elegantly cut. The jacket had this slight flare. She swept her hair into a bun and clasped a pearl necklace from their fifth wedding anniversary around her throat. Daniel came home and she served him rosemary lamb and chocolate nut truffles, all bought at the gourmet food store with one hundred dollars of her money. Re-invest for greater profit later. She did not eat, but massaged his shoulders, and brought him coffee and when he seemed calm and satisfied, she sat down with him at the table.

"You're being so loving," he said. "What a week we had, didn't we?" He warmed his palms against the mug.

"And you look great in that suit, Janet," he said. "Like one hot businesswoman."

She brought a piece of paper onto the table. And then nodded, as if to signal herself to begin.

"I know it's odd," she said, with no introduction, "but for whatever reason, I can't seem to summon up any desire right now to do it without payment." Her voice was the same one from the lingerie store when she'd walked out with the bustier on. "I need a specific amount, each time," she said, "or," clearing her throat, "I feel I will melt into nothingness." She adjusted the cuffs of her suit jacket so that the buttons lined up right with the gateway into her hand.

"What's that paper?"

"Just for notes."

"Are you going somewhere later?" he asked, sipping his coffee.

"Did you hear what I said?"

"I'm getting to that," he said. "You're just all dressed up, I was trying now to figure out why."

"I'm not going anywhere," she said coldly. "I dressed up for you."

He replaced his coffee in the center of the small white napkin. "Well, you look very nice," he said. "As usual. But Janet," he said, "please, will you tell me why, more money, why? If it's to please me, I am so pleased. You and I had a wonderful time this week and I will remember it forever."

"Me too," she said, nodding. "Forever."

"But then why more money?" he asked, moving his chair closer to her. "Wasn't it just a game? Don't you like our sex? Isn't sex its own reward? What can we do differently?"

He reached out his hand, warm from cupping the mug, and placed it on her collarbone, tracing the line with his finger.

"It's good," Janet said briskly, "I like it, I like how you touch me on my back, I like the pace and I like it." Daniel moved his finger to the dip at the hollow of her throat, but her voice did not shift or relax. "But Daniel," she continued, "let me make something clear. Maybe you did not know this, but nothing is its own reward for me." She stared near his face as directly as she could. The words felt like fireballs in her mouth. "I want you to understand that. You don't have to understand why, just that it's true."

"That nothing is its own reward? Really?"

She sat up straighter. "Now, we can of course reduce the fee to make it more financially feasible. Fifty?"

He took his hand off her body and placed it back on the table. "I mean, Janet," he said, "do you have any idea how hard I am working my ass off to make—"

"Twenty?" she said. "I know you're working so hard, honey, I know. But it would mean so much to me." As soon as her voice softened, it began to break apart. "I can hardly explain how much it means to me."

"Twenty?" he said. "Twenty?" He stuck out his lower lip, thinking. "Twenty? Jesus. I suppose I could do twenty for another week but I don't like it. I don't want to. And is nothing its own reward, Janet? Really? Isn't love its own reward?"

"Or thirty?" she asked, sorry now that she'd gone so low.

"Twenty, Janet," said Daniel. "And then come on now. How much money can you really make in a week off twenty dollars? Do you have something you need to buy and don't want to tell me about? Do you think you should reconsider going back to work?"

"Twenty-five?" she murmured, tears in her eyes.

He sipped the last of his coffee very slowly, and when her eyes spilled he leaned in to kiss her forehead. "Twenty-five," he said. "Fine. Until November 1, though, and then we're back to regular. Okay?"

"November 8?" she asked, brushing dry her cheeks.

"*Janet!*"

She moved closer and pressed him desperately to her. "Our love is wonderful," she said. "I know that. I know it's true."

His nose pushed into the smoothness of her hair. "We're each other's reward," he offered, but she just dug her head deeper into his shoulder and whispered blanks into the caves of his neck.

"November 8, then," he said. "And that's it-it-it."

"Thank you, Daniel," she breathed. "You have no idea."

After they hugged, he went to watch TV. She wrote it all down carefully on the paper. November 8. 25 dollars. 770 currently. As if she would forget.

«» «» «»

Starting the next morning, she initiated sex every day. If the week before had been largely his fantasy enacted, now it was all hers. In the shower, in the darkness under all the covers of the bed, at his storeroom among the shoeboxes in his workboots. It felt slightly pathetic to her that she had to do four now to each one before to make the same amount of cash, but she was ravenously hungry for contact all day long and Daniel, who had grown accustomed—before the previous week—to a steady but slightly lackluster sex life, let her enthusiasm spark his own. He took several lunches with Edward as a break, and only begged fatigue a couple times when Janet's demand was kind of overwhelming, he said, since he'd just gotten home and just this morning in the shower and he needed some food and couldn't they watch TV tonight?

She laughed with big red smudge-free lips and fed him and bathed him and let him watch four sitcoms in a row, but before he fell asleep she was on him again and said he didn't have to do anything at all but just be still and sleepy and she would complete all the movement.

At the end of the week, on Sunday afternoon, she presented him with a tidy bill, type-written, accounting for each time, and labeling where/when it had happened, with a dotted line and a $25 at the end. The total for that first week was $250. A small amount compared to the easy near-thousand of the previous week, but a clear exchange nonetheless. Daniel paid it into her palm, in cash, counting backwards. "Sunday's my day off," he said, when she started to undo her bra. "Go do something else, honey, please." He plopped in front of the TV with a bowl of rice cereal to watch some football. Janet gathered herself into the pale blue bathtub and attended to her body quietly in there, moaning softly under the whir of the bathroom fan; afterward, she paid herself $50 by transferring funds from her savings to her checking account. That made $300 for the week.

《》 《》 《》

November 8 shot around the corner in a blink; it was probably the quickest two weeks of her life. And it was not enough. That much was clear instantly. She had started, by now, to see the entire world in terms of currencies. She considered charging her few friends for their lunches based on who demanded more, charging strangers a quarter in the supermarket aisle when they did not move their cart in time. Charging for each meal she cooked, including tip. One afternoon, when her father sailed off into one of his long monologues on the phone, she actually tape-recorded their conversation and then took four hours and typed it out as a script, with his endless speech on the right side of the page and her responses on the left: yes, uh-huh, of course. It was amazing to see the contrast. How long were those reports. How little she spoke. How wealthy she would be if she just charged him a dollar a word.

I am twenty-four hours resentment, said Janet, in her bustier, to the glinting mirror. I am every-cell resentment. I am one hell of a big resentment, she said. The mirror and wall did not answer. They knew very well what she was like by now. But when had it shifted? In high school, she'd walked tall in her own deprivation and had volunteered at the homeless shelter for fun. She bought her dad charming birthday gifts and the homeless shelter made her a mobile saying she was wonderful, with each paper letter brightly colored, hanging from the stick. The N and R fell off in a week, so over her bed, for years, the stick turned slowly, announcing WODEFUL. I am grateful, she'd said every day in high school, grateful for the food on my plate and the roof over my head. Grateful for my dad. Grateful I live in a country where we have options. For our beautiful environment, she said on Saturdays, sorting through the sticky plastic bottles at the recycling center.

Now, years later, even washing a single dish irritated her. I do everything around here, she grumbled to herself while moving the sponge over the circle. Even though she knew it wasn't true. She hadn't done the dishes in weeks. Daniel changed all the lightbulbs and paid the bills. He rubbed her feet and listened to her complaints. The truth was, she just didn't want to do anything at all. She did not want to have a job or have children or clean the bathroom or say hello. She only did a dish with happiness just after Daniel did a dish. She only bought Daniel a present after he'd just bought a present for her, and even then, she made sure her present wasn't quite as good as his.

It disgusted her as she did it, but it was the truth. She certainly liked the image of herself as the benevolent wife with arms full of flowers, but if she bought the flowers she would spend part of the ride home feeling so righteous and pleased that she had bought flowers; what a good wife she was; wasn't he a lucky man; until by the time she arrived home with the flowers, she'd be angry he hadn't bought her flowers.

She reached out a hand to touch the cool sweep of the wall.

"It seems," she said to it, "that I have lost my generosity."

Her whole body filled with a sparkling panic, painful and visceral as poison champagne, as she did not know how to get it back.

‹› ‹› ‹›

The grand total on November 8 was $1270. Daniel paid her the money and gave her a fake sad look that could not disguise its relief, and then trundled off to the bathroom to get ready for work. He was tired. He missed Edward. She ironed the new bills and packed the grand total into her tiny pocketbook of black velvet with the glittery clasp. The cash poked out its green fingers and her heels made pointed bites in the cement as she walked down the street, past the stores. She kept opening up the clasp of her purse and sticking her hand in there and stroking the money like it was a fur glove or a child's hair. What with the angle she held her bag and that look on her face, to other passersby it seemed vaguely like she was masturbating.

People looked away. It was either that, or stare. She was magnetically disturbing to watch.

She stopped when she reached the mall, big and curvy. She roamed the three floors and mingled with all the people milling about with their big paper shopping bags and worn drawn faces.

Inside the biggest and fanciest department store, at one end of the mall shops, she walked around the various sections of women's clothing and observed all the different desks and all the different sets of salespeople. She watched for an hour, noting how each saleswoman interacted with customers, and how she looked, until she settled on one she liked best. This was in the Women's Impulse department. The saleslady was about Janet's age, and had a red velvet ribbon tied neatly around her neck, just like the horror story Janet had once heard, about a woman who wears a velvet ribbon around her neck her whole life, every second of every day, until the one night when her curious husband removes it and her head falls off.

"Excuse me," said Janet, resting her pocketbook on the counter. "I have a question for you."

"Sure." The saleslady re-upholstered her salesface in seconds. "How can I help you?"

"Do you support yourself?" Janet asked the saleslady.

"Pardon me?"

"I know it's an unusual question, but do you support yourself? Are you self-supported? Financially?"

The saleslady squinched up her nose. "Well," she said. "As a matter of fact, I am. Why do you ask?"

"And do you have a boyfriend?" Janet took in the bare left ring finger. Then she refixed her eyes on that red ribbon. The more she looked at it,

The Red Ribbon

the more it did seem to be glued to the woman's neck, and the red of the ribbon was the perfect shade to bring out the red in her lips and the brown of her eyes. It was the kind of glorious and simple fashion move you could stare at for hours in admiration.

The saleslady laughed, uncomfortable. "I'm sorry, are you looking for clothes, ma'am? These are fairly personal questions. There's a sale on long skirts on the right."

"But do you?"

"Why?"

"I'll look for clothes in a second," said Janet, "I need a cream turtleneck. Ribbed. Wool. Expensive. I'll need two, maybe three. But I'm just curious. Do you?"

"Well, yes," said the saleslady.

"Then please, let me just ask you this little bit more," Janet said, leaning on the counter. She hugged her pocketbook into her chest.

"When you go out to dinner," she asked, "who talks more?"

The saleslady squinted at Janet, and then relaxed against the cash register. Business was slow; only a few other customers rotated around the perimeter of the department.

"You mean during dinner?" asked the saleslady.

"Yes."

"Depends on who has more to say that day, I guess."

"And who pays?"

"We usually split it," said the saleslady. "We both make about the same salary. Or one will take the other. There's no rule. What kind of turtleneck? You might want sportswear instead, that's one floor down. Did you say wool?"

Now, in addition to the ribbon, Janet noticed how the delicate mole punctuating the tip of the saleslady's eyebrow looked just like Venus, at the tip of a crescent moon. Perfection.

"And do you regularly orgasm?" asked Janet.

"Excuse me?"

Janet held still. She could hear the cash registers erupt into sound around them. Printing out receipts over the sounds of pens signing shiny credit card paper that curls into itself.

"Please," said Janet. "I know it's very forward, but please. It would mean an enormous amount to me to know."

The saleslady's eyes dodged around the store.

"The turtlenecks are downstairs," she said. "You'd better go down there. There's a woman downstairs in that department who likes to talk about things like this, you should ask her. Molly, look for Molly." Janet shook her head. "I want to ask you," she said.

The saleslady was fidgeting all around the cash register now, pushing buttons, ripping tissue paper, as if she were trapped in there.

Janet took a breath. "Look," she said. "I seem crazy, but I'm not. I just don't know what it's like for other people. Do you keep track? I live a sheltered life. I don't want to ask Molly because I'm not like Molly, I'm more like you. This will be my last question, honestly."

Janet fumbled in her purse and pulled out two hundred dollar bills.

"I'll pay you," she said firmly.

The saleslady stared at the bills and balled the ripped tissue paper into hard pellets.

"Two hundred dollars?" She glanced over her shoulder. "For one question? Are you serious?"

Janet didn't even blink.

The saleslady's eyebrows crunched in, and the mole pulled closer to her temple.

"And then you'll stop?"

A nod.

"And are you a member of this store?"

Janet fumbled in her wallet again and this time produced a bronze store credit card.

"Well," the saleslady said, nodding tightly, "if it's worth that much to you. Fairly regularly, yes. What would you call regular?"

"Majority of the time," Janet said.

"Fine then," said the saleslady. "Majority of the time. About seventy percent, through one method or another. Easier on some days than others. I don't keep track, no. Better off the pill than on. Nicer for me at night than in the morning. Now. Done! The turtlenecks are that way."

Her face was flushed. The red ribbon matched, in perfect harmony, the blush high on her cheeks.

Janet thrust the bills forward and held herself back from taking the woman's hand and kissing it.

"Thank you." She felt her eyes watering. "You are really very beautiful." The yearning in her voice was so palpable it caught them both by surprise.

The saleslady stared at the money and broke into uncomfortable giggles before she grabbed it and strode off into the suit section. The older, blonder manager meandered over from across the room, sensing a need for managerial skills.

"Can I help you?" she asked Janet, now standing alone at the register.

"I need a turtleneck," said Janet.

«» «» «»

In the horror story, the woman tells the man that she loves him, and she will marry him, but he must never remove the red velvet ribbon around her neck. It is the one thing he can never ask of her. At first it's the easiest trade; he agrees and for years they are blissfully happy, but after awhile it begins, in a slow broil, to burn him up inside. Why all the mystery? He unties the ribbon late at night, while she sleeps, and her head rolls onto the floor.

Before, at summer camp, the story had always made Janet puff with righteousness. What a pushy spoiler of a husband. Wasn't their happiness enough? Couldn't he respect her one rule? But in the dressing room, her nose full of the clean smell of new turtleneck, she felt the story tugging at her. Something she couldn't put a finger on. As she paid for the turtlenecks—three—cream, fuschia, black—she told a quick version of the story to the blonde manager, a woman who clearly knew her way in the world. Strong shoulders, proud large hands, open smile. "What do you think it means?" Janet asked. Far off in the distance, she could see the saleslady of her choice re-hanging blouses on a rack.

The manager flattened out the receipt to sign.

"I remember that story," the manager said, sighing. "I had the cutest camp boyfriend."

"I mean, why not just be happy with the way things are, right?" said Janet.

The manager took the signed receipt and put it in the register's pile. She folded the turtlenecks, separating each with a sheet of tissue paper, and then slipped all three into a bag. "But can you blame him?" she said, handing the bag to Janet. "I mean, I'm all for clothes, but at a certain point, they're supposed to go away, you know? How long were they married?"

"I don't know," said Janet, taking the bag. "Story doesn't say."

"Take it all off!" said the manager. She winked at Janet. "Turtlenecks are good that way too."

Across the room, the woman with the red ribbon finished lining up the blouses and had moved onto the slacks. It was true, what the manager said. The ribbon was practically made to be removed. Even Janet herself wanted to slide over and undo the knot and unspool the choker from the woman's throat. So the man didn't know what was coming, Janet thought, as she walked to the escalator. They'd been married for years, and he wanted her to give up the last thread of cover, so she would stand before him, nude, and he could make love to her entire skin.

Well, of course that made her head fall off. Of course.

«» «» «»

At home that night, wearing her new fuschia turtleneck, Janet made a simple dinner of spaghetti and red sauce from a jar. She and Daniel ate together in silence. When they were both done, he cleared the dishes and put them in the sink.

"Thank you," he said, at the counter. "That was very good."

She watched him run water over the forks. His hair needed a cut—it was getting too long on the sides.

"You know, you were right," she said. "What you said a few weeks ago. About your wife."

He didn't turn from the sink. "When I brought you flowers?"

"Yes."

"And what did I say again?"

"That she does not love you very well."

He ran his finger under the tap, back and forth, and poured a glob of dish soap on the pile. "Actually, I think I said something different."

She picked up the drying cloth. "Oh?"

"I think I said that she doesn't love me at all."

He cleared a dish clean with the sponge.

She leaned over to touch his arm. "Daniel," she said.

She could feel the turtleneck, covering up her neck, her shoulders, her torso. Pants, covering up her legs. Socks, over her feet. Underwear, over her pubic hair. A bra, over her breasts.

"I want to do better," she said, quietly.

He placed the dish carefully in the dishrack, lining the circle up with

The Red Ribbon

the bent wire.

"Do you ever think about leaving?" he asked.

"No," she said.

He turned to her. His eyes were bright. "Sometimes I do," he said.

"Do what?"

"Think about leaving," he said.

She shook her head at him, confused. "But you can't leave," she said. "You're the devoted one."

His eyes were kind, and sad, at the sink. And she could see, suddenly, that they were on their way to leaving already, that this conversation was only walking through a door already open, and once those eyes left, they were not going to return, and the clothing would be no barrier at all, nothing, shreds, tissue, air, for all the pain then rushing in. ◉

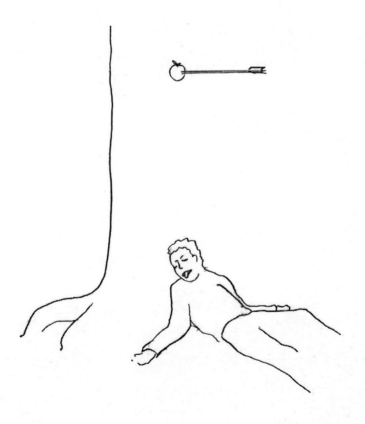

MELL

Little Things

folded my arms. They felt big, capable of anything. Lifting, carrying, digging, feeding cows PCP so they revolt with unexpected and tremendous violence—anything. Wrapping gifts in tissue paper and busting teeth out of Christian heads. Pumping bicycle tires, pumping gas, pumping iron, bagging my own groceries and skipping boulders across the Long Island Sound all the way to Connecticut. Cracking eggs with one hand and folding laundry. Pushing my Mexican neighbor's broke-down car across the street Thursday mornings to avoid street sweeping tickets and tossing my cell phone to a friend who needs to make an important call to his mom. Opening every jar for every lady. Helping. I felt like helping. I felt like I could help.

The first thing I did was clean the microwave. I went from there. Sometimes I succeeded, sometimes there were other times. I've witnessed people break, cry, collapse, kill themselves, get killed, or get old. I've seen people lose their hair, their minds, their driver's licenses. My father lost his gallbladder from dieting with Nutri/System. What could I do? I mopped the kitchen floor, took a walk, saw a dead baby rabbit with a bicycle tire tread through its middle. It reminded me of a friend of mine who had hairy legs and liked fireworks. One summer he caught his girlfriend cheating, sprinted from her doorstep toward Vanderbilt Boulevard, and dove in front of a station wagon with three kids in the backseat.

Matt Sumell   39

I saw an old lady in 7-Eleven wearing a nightgown, with red mittens on her feet and blue veins in her ankles. I bought potato chips. People got married. They got houses and they got furniture and they trusted the government and they got fat. There was a homeless man with long hair, a black leather jacket, green cut-off shorts, and a mental problem that he tried to walk off like a little league baseball injury. Walking, walking, always walking. He was very tan. The locals called him the man with a million miles on his feet. The police shot him in the back when he didn't stop to answer their questions.

I remember sitting in the passenger seat of my father's diesel after a Roy Rogers dinner—I always liked their fixin's bar. My brother was in the backseat. A couple cars in front of us, a car swerved left; then the next car swerved, then the next, until the car directly in front us didn't swerve. We watched in the headlights as three puppies rolled out from underneath it, leaned closer to them as my father braked, steered around and past, and pulled over. On the side of the road two of them looked just fine, except they were dead. The third was bleeding—it was hard to tell from where exactly, there was a lot of blood—but it kept breathing for a few minutes before it stopped and died in the on-and-off orange of my father's hazards.

A grasshopper jumped into a rest-stop toilet. People ate veal. I dated a chubby Catholic girl who told me her parents never touched her, that as a kid she wanted to be touched so badly she looked forward to the lice and scoliosis tests at school. I knew a guy in junior high who told everyone he owned a baby elephant; years later he murdered his stepmother by beating her head in with a can of chicken & stars soup. I saw cats, dogs, possums, raccoons, and squirrels; a fox, a kangaroo, a bear, deer, rabbits, birds, and toads; rats and mice and snakes with their guts smashed out, their insides outside, their heads crushed and dead on sunny roadsides. My mother got cancer.

I came home, held her hand, pushed her pain button, did her nails, fluffed her pillows, brushed her teeth, and emptied her piss bag. I bought her stuffed animals and licorice and long straws so she could drink her juice in bed. She mostly just slept and vomited. Her hospital room was noisy. There was lots of moaning, beds creaking, PCA pumps beeping, nurses coming and going and laughing and asking how are you on a scale of zero to ten, zero being no pain and ten being the worst pain you've ever felt? Twelve.

Three months into it my brother and I were watching the Dilaudid drip, listening to her mumble ow ow ow in her sleep, when her eyes opened wide, then wider, then came back together in a real slow drug-drunk blink. Then she threw her sheet on the floor, picked her hospital gown up over her head. "No more fucking water."

I said, "Do you want me to go to the Coke machine?"

"Why are you trying to kill me?"

"We're not."

"Do you realize I'm laying here, full frontal?"

"Yes."

"Are you happy to see your mother full frontal?"

"Not really."

"Then get out."

We sat there, unsure of what to do or say, where to look. She yelled that there was salt on her legs, something about conductors and the procedure, and don't touch my antique fork. She ripped the IVs out of her arms, the Hickman port out of her chest. Blood shot up in the air. I grabbed her as my brother went running down the hall toward the nurses' station, screaming. I held her down by the wrists, it wasn't difficult, she hadn't been eating, maybe weighed eighty-five pounds at that point. When she was through struggling she just kinda collapsed in on herself and cried. I said *Mom* like it was a question.

Later, after they had strapped her to the bed, bandaged her up, shot her full of strong whatever until she passed out, redid her IVs in her feet so she couldn't reach them; after, we had called our father and lied that everything was fine and he should take the night off, called our sister and told her what happened, then regretted it; we smoked a couple cigarettes out front with a transporter who had burned his hand with cinnamon roll icing, and decided we'd both spend the night. Back in the room, after we sat there watching the Dilaudid drip, not speaking for half an hour, just listening to our mother mumble ow ow ow in her sleep, my brother turned to me and said, "Yo, her vagina's in a lot better shape than I thought it'd be."

I considered it for a second, then nodded in agreement.

She came home to die. Hospice delivered a bed, equipment, boxes of meds, and a lady doctor who said one to three days. We set her up in the den, under the ceiling fan where my sister had tied little glass dragonflies with string. My mother seemed to like watching them fly their circle around the room but I didn't. I got good at spackling, got impressed with bubble gum's resistance to decay, ate her Ativan like aspirin. I told her that I'd miss her, that I hated her body for getting sick, that I wanted to seize God or fate or the universe by the throat and make it leave her alone. She laughed at me. Her bedsores leaked an awful-smelling fluid. My brother, sister, and I took turns changing her bandages and sheets, drank her liquid Valium, and played UNO. We watched our father watch her dying, learned from the grief on his face every time he walked in the room. He never lasted more than ten minutes. A priest came to give her last rites and I gave him my meanest look. He asked me if I'd like to receive communion and I gave him a different meanest look and walked out of the room. A week later, the lady doctor came back, said one to three days. My brother and I wrote each other cheerer-upper notes on brown napkins:

Do you worry that Mom will see your gay thoughts from heaven?

No. Do you worry she gets x-ray vision and sees the undescended testicles in your girlfriend's abdomen?

That girlfriend, Tara, came over later that day and hung around like she was part of the family, then cooked us a chicken for dinner. Just as we sat down to eat it, my brother said I should do the dishes. I said, "You're kidding?" He said he wasn't. I told him that I wasn't gonna do any damn dishes until he cleaned his IBS shit shrapnel off the fuckin' toilet. His face turned red. I said, "Looks like you might wanna hit me. If you do, I'm going to stab you in the head with my fork." Then I took a bite of the chicken—it was pretty good—and he punched it out of my mouth. I was so shocked that I didn't do anything for two whole seconds and neither did anyone else. Then I lunged at him, strangled him, smashed his head into the kitchen counter. He started bleeding from somewhere in his hair, his girlfriend started pulling mine, and my sister wedged herself between us. I think she caught a stray or two before we all fell into the empty beer bottles on top of the radiator. My father came wobble-running in like a gorilla, yelling something I couldn't quite understand because Tara was clawing at my ears.

Outside in the driveway I caught my breath, smoked a cigarette, stomped on a disc of ice frozen into the upside-down lid of a green garbage can, shook. A few minutes later my sister came out with my jacket and asked if I was all right. I said I was and asked if my brother was all right. She said he had a pretty good cut on his head but seemed all right. For the first time in a long time I felt relief, like I had just fucked or cried or quit a job. It feels good to be punched in the face, to punch someone in the face. I walked to the Mexican restaurant around the corner and drank Budweiser. Twenty minutes later my father showed up, said he followed my footprints in the snow. I asked him if he wanted to do a shot of something, anything. He said, "If I start drinkin' now I won't stop." Just then my brother called my phone.

He said, "Hey man."

I said, "Hey man."

"Did you really stab me?"

"No."

"Are you gonna do the dishes?"

"Yeah, I'll do the dishes."

"Cool."

"Is mom still alive?"

"Yeah."

"Cool."

She died a week later. I got a job gutting houses.

I worked with an interesting guy who smoked things off tinfoil; he had a rough childhood and adulthood's rough on everyone. We were ripping vinyl tiles out of a kitchen when he told me that a twenty-eight-year-old girl he knew was working at Lord & Taylor when her heart exploded. He told me just like that, plain, not angry at all. I told him that a fifteen-year-old from Bayport stepped in front of a LIRR train and let it run her down.

"I heard about that," he said. "It dragged her body a mile."

Also, two bicyclists were killed by one car on Sunrise Highway, and a twenty-year-old died of a drug overdose a block away. Her daughter was three. Every year, at least two people drown in Lake Ronkonkoma and thousands of toads drown in swimming pools. A good friend's kid brother got killed in Iraq, a really pretty girl I met once in San Francisco went to sleep one night and didn't wake up, and a guy I know didn't have health insurance when he was diagnosed with Multiple Sclerosis. The restaurant he worked at was kind enough to have a fundraiser for him that grossed over five thousand dollars. They gave him four hundred.

I went to lunch with my family, asked my sister how she was doing since mom. She just looked at me and let her eyes water. I asked my dad the same question, he just pointed to my sister like, "I feel like that." My brother shrugged. I told them that I was okay, which might've been true, that I'd help them if I knew how. The waitress came over, dressed in all black including the apron, called me ma'am, sir … ma'am. I said, "Do I look like a lady to you?" She stammered an apology, said she hadn't looked closely enough, which was strange because she was avoiding looking at me while she spoke. I didn't eat much, picked at my french fries and drank ice water while they ate and argued about money. I didn't know what I thought about money, and I didn't feel like arguing about it. We're not a dessert family but we like black coffee. I was almost done with my cup when my sister said she went to the cemetery and ate some of the grass off our mother's grave. My father reached for his wallet.

When we got home there was a baby sparrow in the driveway, lying there, featherless. It was tiny. Its skin was almost see-through. We were all just standing around it—looking. I said I'll go get something to put it in and started toward the house. My father said maybe the best thing to do would be to back over it with the car. ⊕

Some Contemporary Characters

There

There are things in this taxable and careworn world that can only be said in a restrictive interface with a minimum of characters:

Saw him on OkCupid. Agreed to meet. In his bio he said he had a "different conception of time." And guess what? He didn't show.

I waited for her three days. On and off. True, they were the wrong three days. Went back a week later—to that coffee shop of longing.

Bunch more online dates. All candidates underemployed with big plans. One guy worked in sewage treatment. One guy played sax on the IRT.

The waitress at the establishment used the word "honey" repeatedly. Each time it was a kindness in that lonely urban setting.

No lie: I walk by the place where I was supposed to meet that man, two weeks later, he's sitting there reading a book.

Certain questions relating to human conduct require earnest reflection. The rest of the world is absent for a time. How to explain?

A man more than twice your age who's always late. Rule him out right away, or at least let him attempt to explain himself?

I said, "Old enough to remember that feminine beauty is nowhere apparent in a point-of-purchase glossy containing the word *cellulite.*"

I said, "Young enough to assert a right to text an account, warts and all, from the diner bathroom in case you're a serial rapist."

Willing to play along, if playing along involves a certain idea of language, because we are how we use the tongue now.

The thinning hair and the extra fifteen pounds, sure, but I could tell that from the photo online. He wasn't a total schlump.

A jeans-with-skirt-over-them-type, sort of busty, with three different hair colors, none of them found in nature.

I think he wore an earring at some point, you could see the little divot in his earlobe—how long ago and why?

If she had an ass-to-die-for what did that mean with regard to gender politics, and was I willing to die for an ass to die for?

What did he actually do? Did he actually do anything? Is it only me who stumbles on these guys whose occupation is *daydreamer?*

Proposed another sit-down, four days hence, then drove to Vermont to have my colon cleansed by a harpie with dreadlocks.

I said yes to the date, then hooked up with a co-worker, b/c I could. For the record: the dude with last shift at the Carmine St. bar.

Next I suggested a film by Tarkovsky because I felt that if she could sit through it there might be hope. Instead, the film caused typing.

Dullest movie I have ever seen: made confessional poetry and folk music night at the Student Union sound like big fun, that's how dull.

The suppression of the semi-colon; the inability to avoid the use of LIKE; the overreliance on the simple sentence—ills of the age.

Why agree to a third date? Because I already had plenty of people to go with me when I needed eyebrow piercing.

Sooner or later love is about death, no matter the lover—desire coughs up the rank fumes of death. And so I proposed bowling.

He said, "The shoes are sublime. The shoes recall a semiotics of freight-train-hopping. And, yes, the pins connect us to American folklore."

She said, "The shoes are funky, and they make me want to dance on one of those light up dance floor video game things. Give me a ten."

He said, "I'd say you were the worst bowler ever, but that would be dia-lectical-style analysis, and, well, Hegel is so eighties."

She said, "If I bowl a strike now you have to tell me if you're impotent or if you take Viagra or have benign enlarged prostate."

Maybe he's a life coach, and it'd be just my luck since everyone says I make dumb decisions about things. But I *can* bowl.

An ungodly strike, an indisputable strike, one pin teetering at the right-most margin like chastity itself toppling with a dramatic sigh.

Not that anyone's keeping track but now comes the part when the rules of engagement permit a discussion of human sexuality.

I determined not to gab, and thereby I would be young again, by instead using my lips for what lips are designed for, which is not gabbing.

Kissing a guy with gray hair on the street in front of a pizzeria by a bowl-ing alley and shoving my tongue *way in,* inadvisable?

Contraindicated. Against the code. Breaking most conceivable taboos. Pedophiliac. Bringing waves of guilt. Still, she *was* ardent.

That was it, nothing else, and people kiss every day, and the only difference nowadays is that people try to text while kissing.

Her eyes drifted off. I could see her preparing something witty: "I can't quxhyte reeeaad keybrd cuz my yongue is in somnody's mout."

Actually, I *did* text on the way home and mainly because I knew my roommate was going to get up in my face: Did he kiss old?

Up around 4am sorting and recycling back issues of *The Nation*. A bit more age appropriate than smooching some barmaid?

He called me because, he said, phoning after a date was required. Land lines—so Tracy & Hepburn. I thought: letting me down easy.

She IM'ed me on FB to tell me that her mother had summoned her home for the weekend, she had to go. I thought: met a kid her own age.

My mother is two years older than he is, same age practically. She's already telling me which jewelry is mine when she dies.

Note to self at dawn: S. Spielrein recognized the destructive essence of longing, an idea she passed on, like an STD, to Freud and Jung.

He's assuming that I get all my information from the iPhone or from the Interwebs. But I also get my info from bar patrons.

Enough! Enough blather! Enough neurotic vacillation! Enough middle-aged hand-wringing! For whatever reason she seems to like you! Enough!

Coney Island was open one more weekend, and it was getting cooler, and I had this halter top I really liked. Cream-colored.

I'd never been to Coney Island, because I dislike crowds, though I had been writing notes about the Russian mob, existentialism thereof.

On the train he told me that his dad, who'd disliked him and called him ne'er-do-well, left him enough money to survive precariously.

On the train she indicated that she'd been assaulted by a friend of her older brother when in her middle teens. Details murky and sad.

On the train he said that his partner of decades, estranged, worked with deaf kids. He saw the loss of her as a "great, enduring fuckup."

On the train she coiled her necklace, some trinket from St. Mark's Place, around her fingers, like a proposition she couldn't resolve.

On the train he said that he hadn't slept with anyone for years. Said his one successful relationship had been with solitariness itself.

On the train she asked what I liked to do with my body, and I winced because there was nothing at all that I liked to do with it.

On the train I asked what he liked to do with his body and he answered that he wasn't certain—how could he be?—that he inhabited a body.

On the train she hooked a thumb in her jeans, and looked away. One sandal and then the other traversed the summit of a knee. I watched.

On the train I tried to flirt, who knows why, because what did I think I wanted? I don't know. Sometimes you just do things.

On the train she could not flirt much because there was no phone service and as a result her affect was much constrained.

On the train I said that the sand was warm at Coney and there were hypodermic needles and if you lay down you could see stars.

On the train I said that I had lower back pain and needed a lot of support under my knees. In fact, I needed support generally.

On the train I looked at his gray pullover, his thriftstore suit pants, his whitish hair. This man will be my lover? And then? After that?

On the train, when the riders thinned out, she circled around the metal pole, mocking and engaging the pole dance.

On the train, when everyone got off, I let him know that I knew what was expected, which was an *idea* of a young woman.

On the train I asked her why she did these things, didn't she have any better way of meeting people? If people were what she was after?

On the train I said why were you on OkCupid in the first place, trolling for co-eds, if you're against the way that people have fun now?

Into an awkwardness of human relations mercy can sometimes felicitously intrude, or, contrawise, we came to the end of the line.

You can see the Cyclone from just about anywhere and my heart thundered at the screams as we ambled off the train.

"You've got to be kidding," said I, "I am no longer young, I am no longer at the point where I can remember my youth, and I'm panicky."

He said: spinning things made him puke, and rollercoasters reminded him of military service, even though he never served.

She said that we were going on the coaster no matter what, even when I observed that the freak show was rumored to be of high caliber.

What's a rollercoaster but a spot where you make out with someone you just mashed yourself against? Is there another purpose?

Entire phenomenon is really about the first great plummet, because every hill after the first is slightly less persuasive.

You have to be willing to do the first hill and to feel the wooden beams of the frame all shuddery beneath you. The rest is gravy.

A price break is offered the second time around, which is the way life is: you pay to be nauseated, then you get a volume discount on *more.*

We rode three times and by the third time the scary parts got all routine, and he was *green,* so we went to play Skee-Ball.

Coney Island is a demolition site, a future overdevelopment shrine, and the only thing that salves the wound is the ubiquity of Skee-Ball.

Roll this old wooden ball up a ramp and try to get it in this ball-sized hole, then you get some tickets which are worth nada.

The tickets are actual tickets, because they say "ticket" on them. If you win ten thousand you can redeem these for a Chinese squirt gun.

I'm good at bowling, and I'm good at Skee-Ball, and so I won a stuffed rabbit, and we took the rabbit and walked out to the boardwalk.

Out there: the same Atlantic Ocean that laps the Outer Banks and pools in Casco Bay. It shimmers in the moonglow, unused.

Every beachfront should have a boardwalk. Every boardwalk should have Orthodox couples. Always there should be gang activity.

I said I was writing about the Russian mob and Dostoevsky for *Contemporary Psychoanalysis.* Wasn't trying to boast. Just talking.

He said he'd like it if we went to have dinner in Brighton Beach because the amusement park was just "too adolescent."

She said I needed to take my "inner adolescent" out and show him a really really really really really really nasty time.

And then we were on the beach, pretty ugly beach with all the trash and everything, but next to the Atlantic. In twilight.

I come from a landlocked state (PA) and I live part-time in a landlocked state (VT) and so I am awed by an oceanic expanse.

I don't want to say that something happened on the beach that wouldn't have happened catalytic. It should have happened on the Cyclone.

I don't want to say that something happened on the beach, that the ocean was somehow responsible, but she did put away her iPhone.

I was supposed to text or e-mail my friend Ariel every twenty minutes or it meant that he was hacking me into pieces and eating me.

Putting the phone in her pocket was somehow the most revealing thing, like when myopics put their glasses on the bedside table.

There was the light from the boardwalk, sound of the ocean, some Latino troublemakers cackling nearby, and we fell into each other's arms.

In the sand. In the sand. I can't even stand up most days, what with the bad back, but I fell into the sand and, oh, her arms!

We twisted around some way so I was on top. For a while. He couldn't crush me. I could feel his complications in the dim light.

She was like some sprite, and there was that incredible feeling, known to all persons, when your cares become insubstantial.

He tasted like Listerine, Mylanta, roast beef, mesclun salad, decaf from one of those old coffee pots from a tag sale, salt water taffy.

She tasted like chai latte, lite beer, nicotine gum, Tic Tacs, grapefruit, cider vinegar, chocolate chip cookies, and the middle class.

He kept trying to say something, but then he couldn't say it. He couldn't say anything. I thought this was amusing.

Low light helps. A distracting milieu. Tens of hundreds of tourists. Calliope sounds. Rollercoasters. The moon.

It'd be interesting to see how many languages, world over, offer some version of the phrase "Get a hotel room!"

They say "Get a hotel room!" in Spanish, they can say it in Russian, and they can say it in, in Black Vernacular Dialect too.

I like saying "Suck my dick" to any asshole who gets on my nerves, but when you're lying on the sand embracing someone you don't bother.

At some point there were limitations which were the limitations of conscience and propriety in a public place, no matter how honky-tonk.

You always think that love or sex or whatever are like totally liberated or totally liberating but there are things you just don't do.

De Sade's only limit was his imagination, you know, but he was in a prison cell when he scribbled down his provocations.

There were a few hotels there, I guess, but we'd have to pay up and he had no credit cards because he didn't believe in usury.

There are certain hygiene regimens—scalp-related—that I really don't like to do without unless it's absolutely unavoidable.

My parents' names are all over my one Amex, didn't want him to see that, and then I realized I didn't have any extra underwear.

So we found ourselves walking back toward the train, upbeat, at least till we realized we'd misplaced the rabbit.

On the train I thought: some feelings you only realize later how important they are. Do you know where your toy rabbit is?

On the train I asked myself, "Am I ready to step out from the wings onto the stage of romantic activity? Did I somehow slay the rabbit?"

On the train he got even shyer, though I'd just felt him up against me, I'd felt his heartbeat and some other parts of him too.

On the train, she knew what I knew, that I was a retiring person trying not to be, and I was embarrassed in her knowing.

On the train it started to feel hopeless and awkward where on the way out it had been hopeful and there'd been an adrenalin of possibility.

On the train, running out of things to say, I figured I'd discuss politics. Must have been desperate, as this is such a bad topic.

On the train he brought up politics, which to him probably meant like Al Gore or something. I was 13 when Al Gore ran.

On the train I stammered about campaign financing being the third rail of the American political establishment and she said: "Huh?"

On the train I told him that I was pierced, I was tattooed, I was tribal, I loved whatever way I wanted to, and that was my revolution.

On the train I said, "You don't understand, politics isn't the kind of thing you can just ignore, even if voting is a big *buzzkill,* and—"

On the train I said, "The other thing you're overlooking, if you don't mind me saying, is tech stuff, and that is *so* political."

On the train I said, "There's a reason that I have failed at all of this sort of thing for years, and I don't want you to have to—"

On the train I said, "Doesn't it occur to you to give a person a chance? Does it occur to you that a person could be different?!!"

On the train I said, "I can tell you are going to use multiple exclamation points when you write this down, and while I admire excess in—"

On the train I said, "This is really stupid, we were having a nice time, and now it's all... I really think it's you."

"Of course you think it's me," I said on the train, "because when does someone your age take on the responsibility for her—"

"You were just waiting to condescend," I said on the train, and I got up and moved to the other side of the car.

On the train I thought: I just held this woman, this china vase, this wolverine, and now I'm no better than the vagrant in the two-seater.

There's a point when you can start repairing all the awful shit you said, but then you kind of dig in and say more awful shit.

I was a social worker at a halfway house back when and I used to say to clients: when you are becoming angry you are becoming reverent.

Sometimes I think that when I am flipping off some asshole, hating him, belittling him, maybe I'm honoring him too.

What if I'm just not in a place anymore when I can go through with it? What if the use-by date is used and bygone?

On the train I said, "I figure you are trying to be nice and you just don't know how, because all you really know about me is my bio."

She was rather vehement about my non-awareness of her unique properties, from across the car, and I was nodding in agreement.

All this had happened, and we still had like, I don't know, eight stops or something. I just had to sit there with him staring at me.

We fitted in the whole of a May to December romance—from unwarranted optimism to contempt—between Surf Ave and Union Square.

I couldn't believe he was willing to write the whole thing off so easy, and now he was going back to his hovel to pick his scabs.

I couldn't believe she wasn't mature enough to realize that this is what happens when you're involved with other people: rollercoastering.

I couldn't believe I rode the train all the way to Coney Island and back with this geezer just because he could quote from philosophers.

We got off the train together, and that was a heavy labor. Another Saturday night in which I was to lay myself down beside insomnia.

We got out, climbed the stairs, he was going south, I was going east. We were alike: both guilty of thinking more than we were admitting.

All I could formulate was the perception that I hadn't really kissed anyone like that in so long. Did I not deserve it just a little?

He said, "We could just start the conversation over as though we haven't met. You could even play my part. It's a small effort."

But then we were kissing good night, and I didn't know why except that this is the custom. Like Judas summoning the Roman guard.

I kissed him good night because I was kissing goodbye to all the old guys and their nostalgia and shaky confidence and felt tip pens.

"I'll call you," I said, which meant, I think, that I devoutly wished to call, but that something was likely to prevent me.

"I'll call you," he said, which meant, I guess, that he wouldn't call at all, but he thought he should say something.

Ninth Street, it was, when she turned east toward the park, and I could see her receding, an actual person receding.

No one would have thought I ever knew him, except that maybe I walked his dog for him or something, or typed his correspondence.

No one would have ever thought I knew her, except from Casual Encounters on Craigslist or because I needed help with my affairs.

I watched him head into the crosswalk and almost get run over by a bicyclist, and then I called Ariel and told her that I was in one piece.

I watched as some fellow accosted her on the sidewalk—for loose change, I suppose. In that moment I seethed with jealousy.

Ariel said I needed to get right back on the horse, the dead horse, so first thing I did was sign on OkCupid. Any activity?

I knew she was going to *post* about it. I decided it wouldn't be the actual mutual-assured-destruction account unless I posted too.

Started following his status updates, because I needed to vet them, you know, but also because I was curious. I mean, they were about *me.*

I'd already friended her, and I confess I felt sad when reading her posts, though can you really be sad about a bunch of ones and zeroes?

Like a week later I saw him through the window in that coffee shop. Looking at his watch, contemplating his different conception of time. ●

This story was originally serialized via Twitter on @ElectricLit from November 30th to December 2nd, 2009.

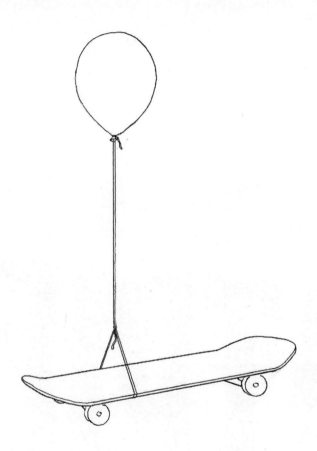

PATRICK

DEWITT

Reed & Dinnerstein Moving

It was Reed's wife's idea that he and Dinnerstein should start a moving company. Reed feigned enthusiasm, but in truth was hopeful the inspiration might vanish, as so many of her other inspirations had. Then she found them a job and rented them a truck, unfolding the cash on the agency counter as though the bills might burst into flames. Now here they were, two men driving along at dawn, stunned by the turn of fate. It was early for them, and sleep clung heavily to their faces. Reed suggested their infant business was in need of a slogan.

"*When The Best Is Just Too Good*," Dinnerstein said, burning his thumb as he checked the truck's lighter. He lit a cigarette and fanned his hand. "*Blood Shed Daily*."

"Are you all right?"

"*The Empathetic Moving Company*."

Reed rolled down the window to smell the damp early-Fall air. His face was a likeable one, at least to those who liked him, but he could never be called handsome. He was in his late thirties and had been friends with Dinnerstein since high school. Neither had accomplished much in terms of moneymaking, mainly because neither had tried, until now. Previously they had labored, clerked, telemarketed—torturous advances into a world they were sincerely revolted by. Reed thought of these other jobs and gripped the steering wheel. Certainly this was preferable to the others. "You'll see," he told Dinnerstein. "It'll go along, job after job, then we'll buy our own truck and it's off to the races."

Dinnerstein was the more handsome of the two, masculine in the catalogue-model mold, an amoral (he would say fun-loving), gay man with a general mistrust of and pity for the average citizen. But he liked Reed; they'd always had an understanding on the key issues. They lived in a cold-hearted part of the world, a lonely, densely forested place with a low, gray-black sky.

"What's this?" Dinnerstein asked, exhaling smoke.

A stoplight was out of service and they pulled up short of a cop directing traffic: white gloves, grim-faced, stiff and serious about his work. "Look at this guy," Reed said. "What's he doing, the robot?" Dinnerstein flicked his cigarette near the cop's feet and the cop looked at the smoking butt, then up at the truck. Dinnerstein held his hands together as though praying and gave a slight bow. The cop waved them on, watching them until they were out of sight. They glanced at each other and chuckled. Dinnerstein lit another cigarette and said, "I used to date a guy from around here. He was a cop, as a matter of fact."

"Yeah?" Reed enjoyed hearing about Dinnerstein's homosexual adventures. "Did he have a moustache?"

"He had a shit moustache when I was through with him."

"A shit moustache," said Reed, marveling.

Passing a public park, they saw a little boy knock a little girl off the merry-go-round. The girl lay on her back and the boy jumped onto her stomach, folding her neatly in two. Other children began to swarm and the boy dove into a thicket of bushes; this caused the thicket to stir as though it were laughing.

Reed stopped the truck and looked out the window to check an address. He waved a car past him. The car honked and he gave the driver the finger.

"Tell me we're not lost on our first job, Reed."

"But we are," Reed said. He looked at his friend and smiled.

‹› ‹› ‹›

The old woman, client number one, stood guard on the path to her house, pointing at her watch and crowing. Without a word or any visible greeting, Dinnerstein walked around her and into her house to work. The woman looked at Reed, whose expression offered her little comfort; she hugged herself with spotted, goose-fleshed arms and hurried away toward something.

Dinnerstein came skipping down the steps with a brown ceramic lamp in his hands. "You've got to go look around in there," he said.

"Nice place?"

"No, it's not!"

And it wasn't. Every flat surface was coated in grease and feathers. "Why feathers?" Reed wondered.

"Bunch of birdcages upstairs but nothing in them," Dinnerstein said. The woman passed by the doorway and Reed asked where the birds were.

"Don't you worry about the birds," she said.

"I'm not worried about them, ma'am, just curious."

"We love birds," offered Dinnerstein.

"All you've got to know about the birds is, they're safe and sound."

Reed dragged his hand across the countertop and held up a palm dirtied with grime and feathers. "Shedding devils, aren't they."

"What're you two standing around for? Why aren't you working?"

"We only wanted to know about the birds, ma'am."

"Movers don't need to know 'bout birds."

"*We Don't Know 'Bout Birds*," said Dinnerstein.

"*Don't Ask Us 'Bout No Birds*," Reed said.

"Get to work!" the old lady said, and they did.

«» «» «»

Dinnerstein sat in the truck watching Reed argue with the old woman in front of her new house. There were boxes piled on the sidewalk and porch, but she wanted to finish the work herself. "I've made a decision about you two," she said, and asked them to leave. They were happy to oblige her, but now Reed was having difficulty collecting their fee. The old woman waved her arms and jabbed at her chest, her mouth twisted and lipless. Reed walked away and climbed into the truck.

"Did you get it?" Dinnerstein asked.

"I got most of it."

"What's most of it?"

"She took twenty off for the statuette and twenty more, she said, for the lip."

"Minus twenty a piece, then."

"I broke the statuette."

"And I've got the lip. Fine by me, Reed."

They divided the cash, one hundred dollars each. It was the first time either of them could remember a just payment, where the fee matched the labor, and they were happy, at least temporarily. They drove to the market for a twelve-pack and Reed called from a pay phone to check on his wife. Dinnerstein was drinking in the cab when Reed returned, smiling. "What's the news with Fun Bags?" asked Dinnerstein.

Reed opened a beer and took a comical, dainty sip. "Got another job," he said.

"Bullshit."

"I don't understand it, but it's true. Two truckloads, that's double the money."

"Double the work."

"Double the money. Someone else called for a quote, too."

They pulled away from the market and onto the highway. They were quiet, no radio, just the sound of the road and the wind, beer swilling in the bottle. It was dark and it began to rain and the wipers didn't work. It took a long time to get back to the rental yard, and by the time they arrived they were both thinking the same thing, that if they weren't careful they'd become career furniture movers. They returned the truck and stood at the bus stop in the rain. Reed was holding the custom magnetic signs they'd gone halves on—R & D Moving—one under each arm, and the beers were all gone. As the bus pulled up, Dinnerstein turned to shake Reed's hand, which was out of character and therefore awkward.

"We'll Quit Whenever We Want To Quit," Reed said.

"We'll Give It A Month Or A Week."

"It Doesn't Really Matter."

"Nothing Matters."

"See you in the morning, Dinnerstein."

The doors closed and the bus pulled away. Reed watched Dinnerstein walk down the aisle to the far back seat, giving a Sally Bowles wave over his shoulder as he sat. The bus rounded the corner, leaves swirling in its wake, and Reed looked up and down the dark highway. The rain had stopped and the air smelled of turf and wood smoke. Directly above him, a street lamp clicked on; the sound made him jump and he laughed. With the signs under his arms he cast the shadow of a bird-man, and he flapped his wings in the artificial light.

They went to the movies to celebrate a month in business, a thousand dollars in each of their bank accounts, with three clients lined up and more calling in every day. Reed was wearing his new Carhartt coat and pants: top to bottom denim. Dinnerstein told him he looked like an assembly-line lesbian; Reed said the outfit would last forever.

"Like a stay in Hell," replied Dinnerstein.

Reed was blushing. He had always felt inferior in the wardrobe department, especially compared to Dinnerstein, whose clothes were a perfect fit.

"I said I'd come along with you," Dinnerstein told him.

"Yeah. I don't know." Dinnerstein wasn't exactly flamboyant, but any discerning clerk would peg him, and despite Reed's disinterest in sexuality he was not prepared to have a gay man picking out his clothes for him in public.

"We could always go to Seattle, if you're looking to… *blend in*."

"It's not that," Reed said, his color flaring up again.

Dinnerstein took pity on him. "We'll shop online, how's that."

Reed nodded. He paid for the movie, hoping Dinnerstein wouldn't speak (what if the cashier thought they were on a date?), and at first he didn't, but then he picked up on Reed's concern and took offense. As they were ordering their snacks, he slipped an arm around Reed's waist. Reed tried to move away but Dinnerstein clamped his hand to Reed's hipbone and told the cashier, "It's our anniversary." Reed watched the pained expression on the teenager's face and blushed a third time. Dinnerstein grabbed the food and skipped away to the theater. They sat in the back row. Reed stared at the black screen.

"Are you mad?" Dinnerstein asked.

Reed dabbed his forehead with a napkin. "That was a bad one."

"Eat a bit of chocolate. I think you're having a heart attack."

A redheaded woman in her fifties sat two seats down from them, smiling in greeting. They smiled back and Reed placed a Whopper on his tongue, a pearl in an oyster. "I just wish you'd go easy on me sometimes, that's all," he whispered.

"Easy on *you*?"

"Yes, me. Some of us aren't unembarrasable."

Dinnerstein munched a mouthful of popcorn. "I sleep with men,

Reed. Deal with it or fuck off out of my life." The woman rose from her seat and moved away. Reed looked up at the sparkling stucco ceiling and emitted a brief, shrill whistle. A moment of silence passed and Dinnerstein said, "Wait a minute, goddamn it, I had a story to tell you, only now I can't remember what it was." The lights dimmed and he jabbed Reed's arm with his elbow. "Movie's starting, movie's starting!" Going to the movies was Dinnerstein's favorite thing to do.

Halfway through the opening credits a large, bearded man entered the theater pushing a woman in a wheelchair. Reed and Dinnerstein watched as he lifted her from the chair, carrying her like a baby to the center row. There was an explosion on the screen and the woman made a loud, nasal sound, something like the call of a goose. "Oh, great," said Dinnerstein. Another explosion and the woman made the sound again, louder this time—so it was for the rest of the film. Whenever there was a scene depicting sex or violence, the goose sound followed. The bearded man hushed the woman, placated her with his hands and whispered pleading words in her ear, but she could not be contained. She would make the goose sound and Dinnerstein would laugh and Reed would blush, growing ever damper with sweat. Two hours passed in this manner. After the movie, in the lobby, Dinnerstein asked the woman, now returned to her wheelchair, if she'd had a good time. Her face was contracted and spit-covered and she looked as though she were being tortured by unseen forces. She bleated in what Dinnerstein took to be the affirmative and the man wheeled the woman away. Dinnerstein shuddered. "Think of all the poisonous semen in the world, sloshing around in the balls of Man."

"Let's get a drink."

"Dutch?" asked Dinnerstein coyly.

They walked down the road to a pub. The woman working the bar said she'd heard the movie was a hoot. "A honk," Reed said, ordering up a double. Later, sitting at their table alone while Dinnerstein was in the men's room, he overheard a conversation between a late middle-aged man and woman on a date.

"What part of the world do you think God enjoyed creating the most?" the woman asked. "Niagara Falls? The Rocky Mountains?"

"Are you serious?"

"The Ganges River?"

"Is this a serious question?"

"I don't know. I guess not."

"You sure?"

"We don't have to talk about anything."

These two reminded Reed of something, a movie he'd seen maybe, a television show—but he couldn't place it. It was an uncommonly sad conversation, one that he felt both lucky and unlucky to have heard. The pair stood up and the man helped the woman into her coat. He paid the bill and held the door open for her; Reed would have thought them lovebirds if he hadn't already heard them speaking. Dinnerstein came back from the men's room and followed Reed's sightline. The man was helping the woman into his car, a Cadillac. "Somebody's going to get the high hard one."

"I don't think so," Reed said.

"They remind me of something."

"They do?"

"But I don't know what."

"The woman asked the man what part of the world he thought God enjoyed creating the most."

Dinnerstein looked wounded. "She did *not* say that."

"I heard it myself."

"I hope he vomited on her."

"He did, basically."

"What other answer is there to a question like that?"

"I guess."

"I hope she dies. Tonight."

They finished their drinks and called for another round. They finished these and called for more. They were comfortable and warm. They had money, and were good friends, glad for the company. Reed smelled his bourbon and said, "I can remember the... *stench*... of an alcoholic parent. I can remember coming home once, it was raining, and I was just a little boy—"

"Wait, shit, now I remember the story I wanted to tell you."

Reed cleared his throat. "Oh. Okay."

"Sorry I interrupted, but I'll just forget it again if I don't..."

"Go ahead," Reed said.

Dinnerstein pulled himself up in his seat and folded his arms on the table. "Well," he said. "Do you remember when I had to go get our check from that wattle-necked woman? She was staying in a hotel while her new house was being fumigated?"

"Mrs. Pearl."

"Mrs. Pearl," Dinnerstein nodded. "She was holed up at that fancy waterfront place attached to the casino, you know? And I must have called the bitch ten times that day but she kept putting me off, putting me off, finally I said, Look, I'm coming down to pick up the check now, all right? And she agrees but tells me to hurry up because it was ten o'clock at night and she wanted to get some sleep."

"You picked up the check at ten o'clock at night?"

"She was a slick little pig, Reed. I had to pin her down."

"But ten o'clock?"

"The story doesn't have anything to do with her, okay? Now listen. It's quarter to ten and I'm heading towards my door to leave and there's a knock, and who should it be but my creepy Thai neighbor, Lu. Nasty little shirtless queer, wouldn't touch him for the world, but he's got a joint in his hand, and without thinking I take a hit. Don't give me that look. My dealer disappeared and I hadn't had any weed in weeks. Anyway, I'm halfway to the casino when I realize I'm way too stoned to be out of doors. I don't know what that stuff Lu gave me was, but—blastoff."

"You did *get* the check, didn't you?"

"Hush, Reed, listen. The bus drops me at the casino, and the parking lot's a zoo of cars and wailing drunk people—it's Saturday night, and I'm just crippled, okay? I'm seriously considering turning back. In fact, I'd decided to do just that when I spy, through the glass doors, Mrs. Pearl sitting at a slot machine, waiting for me. So, fuck it, right? I buck up, and I'm walking towards the entrance when I see something awful, which is what looks to be a child in the cash cage."

"What's the cash cage?"

"The big glass box filled with dollar bills? It's a popular casino attraction. There's a high-pressure fan attached to its side that swirls the money around. People pay to stand inside there for sixty seconds a go. Whatever they grab they get to keep."

"Sounds depressing."

"Even more so when you're high and there's a nine-year-old boy inside it. He was really going for it too, leaping up and down, and there was a crowd of people watching him scramble around and they were all hooting at him and banging on the glass—it was a living nightmare."

"I think I would have left."

"I was going to! I thought, *life's too weird, Dinnerstein, and it's time to go home.* But then Mrs. Pearl sees *me*, and starts waving, and I *have* to go inside. So, shit. I hike up my pants and push though the doors and the noise is overwhelming, lights overwhelming, and I tell myself not to look over but I can't help it, I look at the kid in the cage and now I see he's not scrambling around trying to get *at* the money, he's frantically trying to get *away* from it. He's terrified, tears are streaming down his face, he's hyperventilating. The child had been put in there by his parents or uncles or whatever, all of them drunk, insane. They were torturing the kid, Reed. By the time his sixty seconds were over he was curled up in a ball, mute. They had to pull him out of there forcibly, leaving a trail of bills as security led the group out the door."

"Then what?"

"Then nothing. That's the story. The kid'll probably never recover. He'll never handle cash in his lifetime."

Reed blinked. "You got the check, though?"

"Yes, Christ. I sat at the slot machine next to Mrs. Pearl's, blew through twenty bucks in five minutes, got the check, and left." Dinnerstein looked around the pub. It was closing time. "But you wanted to talk about how bad your Dad smelled?"

"I don't want to anymore," said Reed.

Dinnerstein yawned. "What's the tally?" he called to the bartender. She didn't answer but began rooting around for her calculator.

«» «» «»

The next morning, on the way to work, there was a blockade at the Agate Pass Bridge, a half-dozen squad cars, a fire truck, and an ambulance. Reed motioned a cop over; the man clomped towards them. It was raining and he was wearing a black slicker. "We got us a jumper," he said. "Huddled in the rafters, see?"

"We're late for a job," Reed said. "If there's any way we could squeak across, you'd be doing us a big favor."

"Impossible."

"But the road's wide open," said Dinnerstein.

"Truck could spook him."

Reed stood up in the cab and looked over the bridge at the waterline.

"Doesn't seem high enough for a suicide."

"It's not. But if he goes in, we go in."

"You personally?"

"No. The royal we."

Dinnerstein shook his head. "The royal we *is* you, dear."

The cop stared. "You can turn around or you can wait, boys. That's the extent of your options this fine morning." He rejoined the huddle of cops and someone handed him a cup of coffee. In a moment the entire group had turned to stare and smirk at Reed and Dinnerstein. Reed blushed and looked away; Dinnerstein began working his nails with an imaginary emory board. The cops laughed at this. The jumper started flailing from his perch and they ran off to watch. "Fun bunch of guys," said Dinnerstein.

"It seems like a pretty good job, actually. They just give you a gun and a car and wish you good luck."

"Freedom to move," Dinnerstein agreed. "They look like giant gumdrops in those slickers."

"What should we do?"

"Might as well wait." Dinnerstein opened a newspaper to the Business section. Reed took the Life and Arts and crossed the street to a portable toilet, left over from a road crew. He crossed back, using the paper to shield his head; it was raining harder now, the jumper still camped in the rafters. Reed commented that there must be some effective, inexpensive way to cover the waste in portable toilets. "What a sight. It's like Bandini Mountain in there."

Dinnerstein was reading the Local News. "I think it's healthy to look at the odd shitpile," he said. "Keeps you grounded."

"You would think that."

"What's that mean?" Dinnerstein folded the paper on his lap. "You think because I'm queer I'm a shit freak? That we're all shit freaks?"

Reed laughed it off, but deep down he wasn't so sure. "What about your ex? The cop?" he asked. "The moustache?"

"That was a joke."

"Was it?"

Dinnerstein reached for the front-page news and said, "I had a dream about you last night. You showed up late to a party wearing a ring of dead bald eagles around your neck."

"Bald eagles? Newly dead?"

"They weren't warm, but they were clean."

"I wonder," said Reed.

"Should we turn back? I'm getting sick of—"

"Look, look!"

The jumper was standing now, disrobing atop the bridge. He was young and white, handsome, blonde, crazy-eyed. He removed his pants to reveal an abnormally large organ. "Don't jump!" Dinnerstein said, "I can make you famous!" The jumper took off his shirt; tattooed on his stomach was a large black swastika. "Jump! Jump!"

The man did jump, though half-heartedly, ping-ponging through the rafters and crashing to the ground near the edge of the bridge. The cops were running around, coffee flying through the air. The jumper was loaded into an ambulance and Dinnerstein groaned when they wrapped him in blankets. "Did you see the pole on that baby?"

"Nazi pole."

"Still. Wow."

They'd been waiting for over an hour and now they didn't want to go to work. Reed turned the truck around and called the client from a gas station pay phone, explaining about the suicide attempt. "Frankly, sir, we're a little shaken up from the sight of it. I'm sure it's on the news, if you wanted to… No. All right. Tomorrow, then. Yes, first thing. Thanks for understanding. I just want to spend a little time with my family, that's all. God bless *you*. Yes. Bye-bye."

"What now?" Dinnerstein asked.

"Let's keep the truck. One day over won't sink us."

"But what do you want to do?"

"I don't want to do anything."

"Bowling?"

"*You* want to go bowling?"

"I don't know. Sure. Why not?" Dinnerstein looked out the window at the parking lot. It had stopped raining and the sun had come out, steam rising from the concrete. "Life," he said.

Reed started the truck. "Bowling then? Or not bowling?"

"I don't know what." Dinnerstein was looking at himself in the side-view mirror. "I could always go home and fuck Lu," he said.

At any rate, they did not go bowling.

For a week, they didn't work because Dinnerstein said he needed a break. Then he showed up for Thanksgiving dinner with Lu on his arm. Reed answered the door and for a moment did not recognize his friend. Dinnerstein's gaze was evasive and he was unshaven. He was not drunk, but looked to have been drinking in the general sense. Reed said, "You should have told me you were bringing someone."

"Why?" Lu stood behind Dinnerstein, peering over his shoulder with ink-black eyes, large and unblinking.

"I guess it doesn't matter. Come in. You're Lu? Well, it's nice to meet you. Dinnerstein tells me you're a fine cook."

"He doesn't speak English, Reed."

Lu stuck his hand out and Reed shook it delicately, ushering his guests into the living room and excusing himself to wash up in the kitchen. He held the hand that had touched Lu's under hot water, watching the meat of his palm turn red.

"Dinnerstein's here?" Reed's wife asked. She was cleaning the wine glasses. Reed stole a glance at her midsection and experienced a slipping feeling. She was not yet showing, but soon would be. "Reed?"

"He's here. He's brought a little friend, too."

"What?" She placed her towel on the countertop. "What little friend?"

"Lu's his name. New boyfriend, I guess. He doesn't speak any English." Reed shrugged.

Reed's wife shook her head and returned to the wine glasses. She had never much cared for Dinnerstein. Reed brought three beers out to the living room and found Lu sitting on Dinnerstein's lap, tickling his chin. Dinnerstein noticed Reed and lifted Lu up, placing him at his side on the couch. Reed was blushing; he was visited by the image of Dinnerstein strangling Lu, and of Lu enjoying it, a visual that made him instantly, righteously angry. He wondered what was happening, what exactly was going on. Dinnerstein pointed to the beers and said, "Don't give Lu *any* alcohol. Not a drop. Trust me on this."

"Whatever you say," Reed mumbled.

"What are you mad about?"

Reed didn't answer. He handed Dinnerstein a beer and drank half of his in a gulp.

"You don't like Lu, that it?" Lu heard his name and perked up. He was stroking Dinnerstein's thigh and Reed wanted to stick his face with a halved bottle.

"I guess I don't," Reed said, finishing his beer and opening the extra.

"Jealous."

"No." Reed was blushing again. "Never mind. I don't know what's wrong."

"Holiday blues," ventured Dinnerstein. He touched Lu's head and Lu arched against it like a cat. Reed returned to the kitchen; his wife found him trembling, staring at nothing, a white spot in his mind.

"The dirty little faggot," he said.

"Which dirty little faggot?" she asked tenderly.

«» «» «»

It was a long, mostly quiet meal. Reed had calmed himself with whiskey and valium. Lu kept his hands on the table and Dinnerstein complimented Reed's wife's cooking, asking for the recipe. She said she'd write it down before they left—she didn't know he was making fun of her, of her life, her notion of happiness, everything. Reed let it slide. It was the first time he could recall his wife and Dinnerstein behaving civilly with one another.

"I suppose Reed's mentioned the big news," she said.

Dinnerstein, laboriously chewing: "No, he sure hasn't."

"Oh, sweetie, tell him."

Reed's eyes were burning and he wanted to lie down, alone. "She's pregnant."

"Well." Dinnerstein mimicked a pregnant belly for Lu, and pointed. Lu clapped and said something in whatever language it was that he spoke. "Lu and I are very happy for you," said Dinnerstein.

"Thank you." She was beaming. "*Thank you, Lu.*"

"Well," said Dinnerstein again, shaking his head, cutting up his turkey.

"What's your problem?" asked Reed.

"No problem." Dinnerstein pointed his knife at Reed's wife. "It's a good thing we started up our little moving business, no?"

Reed's wife said, "Did you show him the cards yet, honey?"

"Cards," said Dinnerstein. "Cards?"

"You didn't show him the cards, Reed?"

"Not yet," Reed answered. His wife jogged down the hall and returned with a shoebox full of business cards. She handed one to Dinnerstein and one to Lu. "See the little moving truck on there?"

"Would you look at that." Dinnerstein leaned over. "Look Lu, look at the little truck. See? The little moving truck?" Lu mimicked a driver turning a steering wheel and Dinnerstein nodded. "That's it. He understands."

"You can carry them around in your wallet," Reed's wife explained. "You can hand them out to potential customers."

"This is all very exciting," said Dinnerstein. "Isn't it exciting, Reed?"

Reed said nothing. He looked down at his empty plate. He couldn't remember eating the food. "I can't remember eating this food," he said. The group offered no response to the statement. Lu began making a clicking sound; his hand dipped under the table and Dinnerstein hummed the opening riff of *Bad to the Bone*. Reed's wife, dabbing her mouth with her napkin, raised a wineglass. "To us," she said. "To our future." Dinnerstein laughed a long time at this. Lu and Reed's wife looked at each other, confused. Reed excused himself and moved to the bathroom. He pushed back his sleeve and bit into his forearm. Drops of blood bloomed in a half moon. He wrapped himself in gauze and tape.

«» «» «»

Later in the month they had a widower client, an older man, gray but healthy—his wife had died from some kind of super-cancer. "It was our house together," he said. "I can't live here alone with her gone." His eyes welled and Dinnerstein, coughing, left the room. Reed stayed behind and consoled the man. "Why don't you go watch some TV, sir. We'll load you up in no time."

"Thank you," said the widower. The sound of football filled the ocean-facing side of the house; Reed found Dinnerstein in the living room, fumbling with his new cell phone. "Goddamn Lu," he said. "Texts me twenty times a day, fifteen cents apiece."

"What's he say?"

Dinnerstein read a few of them aloud:

"DOING LAUNDRY, U?"

"SO HUNGRY!"

"MISSING U!"

"OH!"

"HEY!"

"BIG BOY!"

"Looks like you got yourself a steady," said Reed.

"Steady pain in the ass. He aims to please, though, I will say that."

"Well, let's get this poor guy settled."

It took two hours to load the truck. When they finished, the widower was sleeping on the couch in front of the TV, a picture of himself and his wife on his lap; they were on a cruise, hugging and smiling, wrapped in sweaters and blankets. Looming behind them was a large blue iceberg. It was the saddest picture Reed had ever seen. "Hey, mister. Come on, wake up."

"Oh? Oh?" The widower blinked and started. "What?"

"It's okay. We got the first load ready. Why don't you lead the way in your car and we'll follow along behind you, would that be all right?"

Had the widower been dreaming? He stared disappointedly at Reed. "Oh. Okay." He looked around the box-filled room, at the picture in his lap. He touched it with the tips of his fingers.

"I'll be in the truck," said Reed.

He sat behind the wheel, waiting, not speaking. When the widower came out he waved and pointed to his car, eyebrows raised. "That's right, dumbshit," said Dinnerstein. Reed didn't say anything. The widower's new house was a retired living community; Reed was surprised by how nice the grounds were. "Not cheap," said the widower. "But I couldn't bear it, couldn't bear being alone there."

"I understand," said Reed.

"All I see is her, there."

Dinnerstein groaned and rolled his eyes, and the widower looked at him sharply. Reed asked, "Which room number's yours?" In the truck, on the way back for the second load, Reed asked Dinnerstein what was the matter with him.

"What do you mean?"

"I mean, do you have to give everyone a hard time? The man's wife died two weeks ago and you shrug at him?"

At this, Dinnerstein smiled. It was not a nice smile. It was like seeing a lion smile. "Teeth," Reed said. Dinnerstein looked away. They returned to the widower's house and went back to work. The sun had set by the time they'd finished; Reed collected the check while Dinnerstein waited in the truck.

"Your friend," began the widower.

"I know. Sorry about that, sir."

"He's got himself an attitude problem."

"He's got a lot of problems." Reed folded the check in his wallet and said good-bye. The widower was standing amidst the stacks of boxes and chairs and tables when Reed closed the door. "That guy's got a long night ahead of him," he told Dinnerstein. Dinnerstein made no reply. After the rental yard, they stood at the bus stop, as always, the magnetic signs tucked under Reed's arms. His annoyance with Dinnerstein hadn't abated, but in the interest of keeping things status quo he said, "I think it's about time we started shopping for a truck of our own."

Dinnerstein laughed bitterly. "I don't think so," he said.

"What do you mean? Why not?"

"It's like you said at the start, Reed, we'll quit whenever we want to."

"We're just getting started. What else are you going to do?"

"I've got a few grand saved. And Lu's got some money, too."

"Lu?" Reed said incredulously. "Lu?"

"Yes, asshole, Lu. What's wrong with that?"

But Reed didn't want to fight. He put his hand to Dinnerstein's shoulder, and Dinnerstein stepped back. "Take it easy," said Reed. "Listen to me."

"What?"

Reed sighed. "Work is work. This really isn't so bad. I mean, this is probably as good as it's going to get for us, you know?"

Dinnerstein's bus came around the corner and he stepped up to meet it. He turned before boarding and said, "If that's the truth, you can do me a favor and slit my throat." The doors closed and the driver pulled away. Reed was alone on the highway. In a moment, an out-of-service bus came into view, the word SORRY illuminated in neon above the driver. Reed waved automatically; the driver returned the gesture and flashed a peace sign. "I didn't think it was so bad, Dinnerstein," he said. Finally, Reed's bus rounded the corner and he dropped the magnetic signs on the ground. The bus stopped and he climbed aboard. He knew the driver by sight, the driver knew him, but they were strangers. "The whole thing's wrong and I hate it," Reed said. The driver nodded his understanding, swung the doors shut, and hit the accelerator. ◑

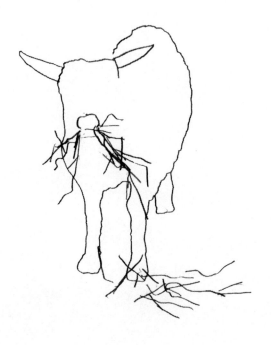

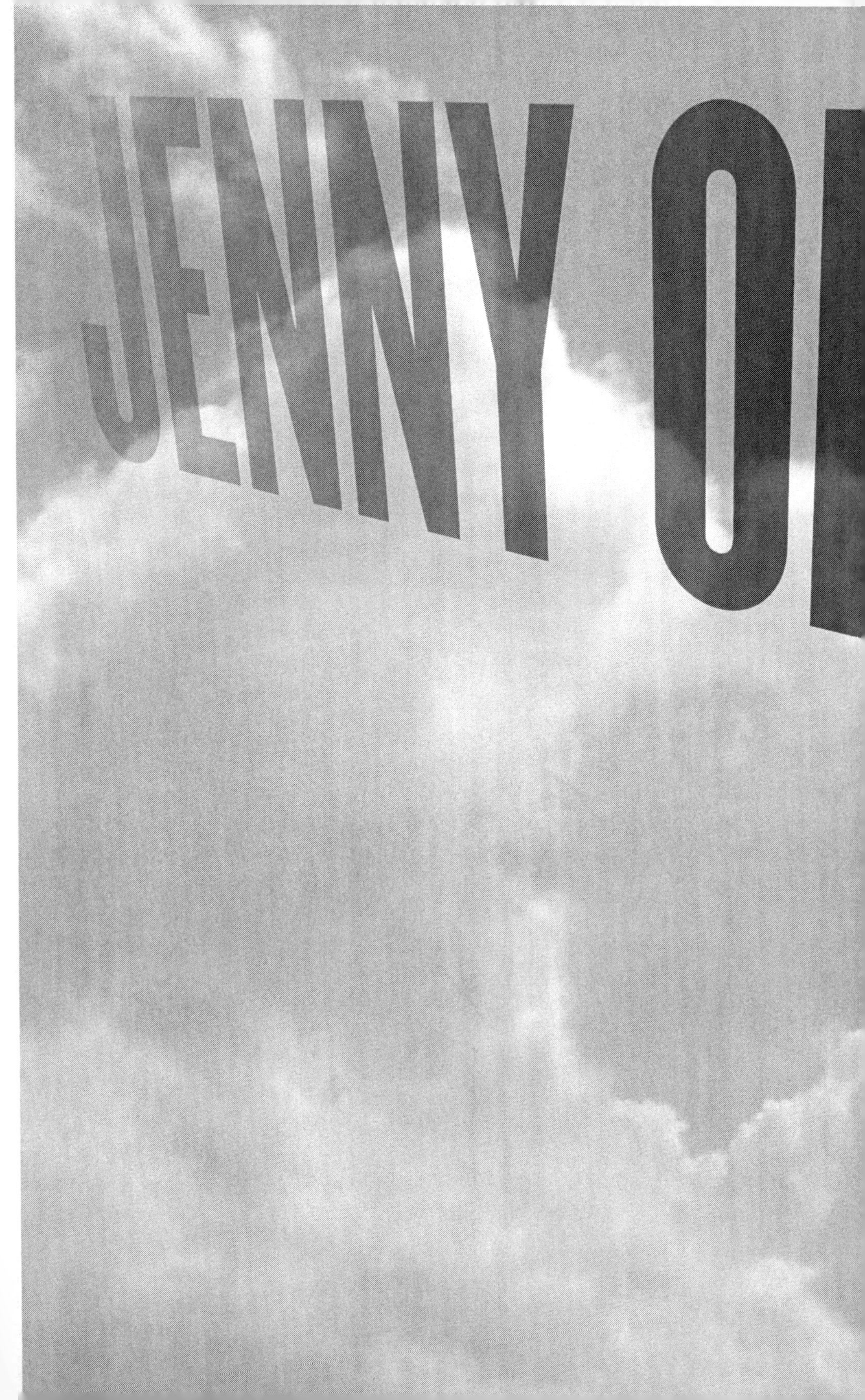
JENNY O

The Tunnel

At first, it was hard to look at her. She had those bright eyes that the dying do. They say time turns hawkish, that you feel it like a wing crossing over you.

He'd read that in a book someone left for Helen. It had a sunrise on the cover. Or maybe it was a sunset. Probably you weren't meant to tell. The book had enraged him, not an ounce of science in it, not a feather of a fact. It was all heaven-hungry, full of soft voices and creatures made of light. Light! As if that wasn't the one thing anyone knew. That it would be dark, dark, dark, with nothing but the earth all around you. "I don't want to be burned," she'd told him years ago. "Don't let them burn me."

So good, a task then. He wouldn't let them burn her. It had been a year and a half since he'd left, but Helen hadn't gotten around to changing her will yet. He was still there listed under next of kin: *Robert Markham (husband)*.

«» «» «»

In the afternoons, he saw Helen in her room. In the evenings, he went home to Sarah. A joke almost, this reversal, but there was no one to tell it to. There was a fat, flirtatious nurse on Helen's floor who allowed him to slip in before visiting hours and it was this kindness that made it possible for him to go there. Of all the people who knew and loved Helen, there wasn't one who would have welcomed the sight of him.

Jenny Offill   91

Most days, Robert came up through a back stairwell which the nurse left unlocked for him. Sometimes he had to wait a few minutes until the hall emptied before going in. That this required a small measure of stealth pleased him. As a boy, he had been the sort who carried a compass and penknife in his sock, who studied which berries were edible and which were poisonous though he'd always lived in Brooklyn. Long past an acceptable age, he had hoped to become an Indian. Instead, he'd ended up a tenure-less professor of biology and though he often thought that he should trap and kill the animals he dissected; so far he had only ordered them through the mail.

For weeks, Robert used the unauthorized stairway without incident. He felt a boyish thrill when he reached the top, as if he had eluded capture by civilized men. Then one afternoon as he was coming up the stairs he ran into Joan Baxter coming down them. She was wearing one of her strange nunnish dresses, black, high-necked, meant for a widow, he suspected. Her hair was pulled back and her face was bare except for a slash of lipstick. His mouth went dry and he remembered the feeling of playing hide and seek as a child, the sudden shame of being found too quickly.

He forced himself to smile and wave. It was the first time Robert had seen her at the hospital though he knew she came there often. Joan was not Helen's closest friend or even her oldest, but somehow she had emerged as the most loyal, she had out-nightingaled all the rest. "Joan, my dear, how are you?" he said as they passed on the stairs, but she only nodded curtly at him.

Robert paused at the railing and listened to the click of her heels descending, then to the sound of the door opening and closing. It was only then that he realized he'd been holding his breath. Shortly after he'd moved out, a postcard had been sent, not to the room he'd rented, but to Sarah's address. It was a plain white postcard, pre-stamped from the post office. *All your friends find you ridiculous*, it said. There was no signature, no indication of who the sender had been, but still he had thought of Joan, of Joan at her desk, printing out the crude block letters.

«» «» «»

He'd had another name for Joan once. Privately, he'd called her "The Poetess". Years ago, when she was in her twenties, she had published a slim chapbook that had been reviewed favorably in a few papers. "Domestic Disturbances", that was the name of it, he remembered. For many years, Joan had tried to write another book, but somehow never managed it. By the time they met her, the whole episode had been turned into a joke of sorts. Joan was purposely careless with the remaining copies, using them as coasters, scribbling grocery lists in their margins. "Oh yes, my brilliant little book, take one," she'd say if anyone asked about it. Once at a party Robert had spotted it on her bookcase and taken it down to look at it. Poems about abortions and vacuum cleaners, that had been his general impression. When Joan saw him flipping through it, he'd gallantly insisted she sign one for him. *From your terribly famous friend, Joan Baxter*, the inscription read.

«» «» «»

When Robert was a real husband, he was the kind who forgot milk, who never picked up the dry-cleaning, who racked up fines at the library even though he drove past it every day on his way to work. But as a pretend husband, he was better. He carried a small notebook in his pocket and kept track of all the things Helen requested, lozenges, tissues, those magazines about houses she always read. Once a week he stopped in the hospital gift shop to get what she wanted. He couldn't manage to go any more than that because he found the store oppressive. It was small and cluttered, full of "Get Well!" balloons and plaques advertising Jesus.

One day as he was buying one of Helen's magazines, he glanced at the calendar behind the counter and saw that it was their anniversary, or what used to be at least. He wondered if he was expected to mark it in some way. He glanced around the store, but everything seemed designed to give offense. The chocolates she couldn't eat, the jeweled barrettes, the inspirational cards touting journeys, not destinations. He thought of their last anniversary together, how restless he had been, ready to hurtle into his new life with Sarah, but not yet brave enough to announce it. There was that fancy dinner at the restaurant where they always went, a carefully worded toast ("To the future," he had said), and more than perfunctory passion, but still she had sensed his imminent defection. "You're looking at me with a cold eye," she'd told him at dinner, and he'd pretended not to know what she meant though the phrase had stunned him with its exactness.

In the end, Robert chose a yellow legal pad and an expensive pen from the meager shelf of office supplies in the gift shop. Helen's throat hurt much of the time now, maybe she could write more, that's what he was thinking as he bought it, but as he stood outside her door with the plastic bag in his hand, it seemed to him that he'd made a grave error. He should be arriving with an embarrassment of flowers or tickets to run away to Mexico together, but instead he had only this paltry offering, like something he had stolen from the office.

"Paper?" Helen said. "We passed that one, didn't we? The paper anniversary is towards the beginning, I think."

"For you to write on," he tried to explain. "To save your throat."

"But what did you give me that first time? Paper, but something funny, I remember."

Robert busied himself with his coffee. Where was his secret stash of creamers? The nurses were always throwing everything away.

"Those printouts!" she said suddenly with a laugh. "That was it, wasn't it?"

Robert nodded. He had, in fact, gone to a great deal of trouble for that particular gift. An old friend at the lab had run their DNA for him and when the papers arrived they had seemed absurdly lovely to him, the little bits that made up their lives printed out together like that. He had folded them into a tiny square and placed them in a velvet ring box for her.

Helen wasn't laughing anymore, but her eyes were still bright with the joke of it. "I remember my friends thought it was the funniest thing. Printouts of our DNA!"

"You said it was romantic," Robert told her. "At the time, that's what you said."

"Did I? I must have thought so then. I remember it came in a box that looked like jewelry."

Something flickered across her face. "Bring me that pen, won't you?" she asked him.

He brought it to her and she pulled herself up from her nest of pillows and began to scribble furiously.

"Bastard," he imagined her writing, but when she handed the paper to him there were only numbers.

"Your mother's jewelry," Helen said. "At the bank. Sarah should have it now."

《》 《》 《》

But later, when he came home with the box of glittering things, Sarah refused to even open it. "Does she have to be such a fucking saint?" she said. "I wish she'd curse us all the way to the grave."

《》 《》 《》

It was a few days before Robert worked up the nerve to give the box back to Helen, but when he did she accepted it without comment, not even raising an eyebrow at him. She was watching a documentary about lemurs. "Beautiful creatures, aren't they?" she murmured. Absently, she touched her head. For a moment, he thought of her hair, how blonde it had been, the giddiness he used to feel when he spotted her in a dark sea of commoners.

Later, on his way out, he saw Joan in the hallway. Her face was flushed from the cold. In her arms, she carried a beautifully wrapped package. Her dark blue coat had a vaguely military air to it. When she spotted him, she gave him a look, the one that meant: you again? He couldn't resist tipping his hat at her. It was the sort of hat meant for tipping, an authentic Greek fisherman's hat that had arrived in the mail just that morning. Robert had ordered it from the back of a magazine, the kind that only advertised expensive things, and the moment he'd put it on he'd felt better, as if there were still adventures ahead of him.

"Joan," he said. "You look well."

"Put your scarf on," she told him. Robert stopped and knotted it around his neck. While he was trying to think of something else to say, she turned and walked away from him.

In the parking lot, he sat in his car, running the engine. He didn't want to go home, but he couldn't think of anywhere else to go either. There was a flyer for a tanning salon on his windshield. Also bird shit. The sky looked weirdly white. Snow, he thought. He switched on the radio to hear the forecast. *Stay in if you can*, it said. An old man called in, worried about his pipes, then another and another. Robert switched the radio off. He decided he'd have a drink somewhere, invent an errand maybe. He had at least an hour before Sarah would be home. It was always better if he didn't go directly to her from the hospital. Better to put some space between them, have a drink first, the same caution he'd employed in the old days.

He set off in the direction of the bar he usually went to, but when he got there, he didn't stop. For some reason, it just seemed better to keep driving. He drove down Tryon, then University, then took a shortcut past the street where Sarah used to live.

McAllister Street. Strange now to think of those early days there. The unplaceable smell of her dim, book-filled apartment. The way the light used to stripe the floor once a day at noon, then vanish. How he'd lie on her filthy couch for hours, swinging dizzily between possibility and despair. The postcard, when it arrived, had seemed oracular. He'd planned to show it to Sarah as soon as she got back from class, but when the moment came, he'd hidden it instead.

They lived somewhere else now, somewhere nicer, but if he tried he could still conjure up every detail of that first awful apartment. The vermin palace, Sarah used to call it, half a joke, half a boast really. There were mice nesting in the oven and a steady stream of roaches that appeared like bad thoughts when you least expected them. Even now, he could close his eyes and see them, their dark brittle shells, the way they fled from the light. *The only life that matters is the life of the mind*, said the magnet on the refrigerator.

Traffic was thinning out now. Trucks, a few last commuters. A light snow had begun to fall. Robert sped up as if he could outrun it, though he knew this was foolishness. As a boy, he had often prayed for snow. It was possible, in fact, that snow was the last thing he had ever prayed for.

He slowed down a little as he came to the edge of town, a long strip of unrelieved ugliness which he had rarely had occasion to visit. The snow was coming faster now. He drove past the used car lot and the dollar store and the liquor mart, each one whitening into oblivion, and then mercifully he was in the country, nothing but woods on either side of him. When he got to the state line, Robert pulled the car over and sat there in the whirling whiteness. He could hear the wind through the crack in the back window. As if in a dream, he saw himself running barefoot through the trees, chasing a deer just ahead of him. Light ruffled its dark fur. His hands were enormous. He realized suddenly that the snow had stopped. It occurred to him to get out of the car. When he did, the cold was like a blow. Robert stood there for a long time, getting used to it. At a certain point, he noted that his feet had turned numb. He wrapped his scarf more tightly around his neck. He remembered that sometimes as a boy he had been so happy that he'd written the word "happy" in the dirt with a stick.

It was getting dark now. The snow was starting up again. People honked and flashed their headlights at him. When he got back inside, there was a deep animal comfort to being somewhere warm and dry again. He started the car and drove back carefully, obeying all the laws he remembered. When he got home, Sarah was waiting up for him. His hair was white, his feet half hobbled. He hadn't been anywhere, he said.

«» «» «»

Spring came and Joan brought Helen lilacs from her garden. She pushed her bed closer to the window so she could see the greening of things. It was impossible to avoid her at the hospital now. Robert had an idea that she must be sleeping there in a supply room or broom closet. How else did she manage to get there before him every day? More often than not, she brought a present for Helen. Robert catalogued these with growing irritation. There was a silver bowl to keep her rings in, a pair of cashmere socks, a clip-on bed light, a jar of hand cream, and a book of jokes for all occasions, charmingly illustrated as if by children.

"What shall I bequeath to Joan?" Helen said one day after she left. "The grand piano? The silver service? The vineyards?" The joke being, of course, that there was nothing really. Nothing except the house which would no doubt be sold to pay off the bills.

"Nothing," Robert said. "Don't give her anything." The words came out more sourly than he intended and Helen paused to look at him curiously. He'd never told her about the postcards though lately there'd been more of them. *You're not fooling anyone with that hat*, the last one said.

"I always thought you liked her. More than my other friends, at least."

Robert shrugged. It was true. He had liked Joan better, liked that there was something sharp-tongued and theatrical about her. She reminded him of the people he had known in New York when he was young, before work and Helen had shunted him off to the suburbs. Right away, they had gravitated toward each other at parties so as to make merciless fun of the other guests. "We're black-

Jenny Offill   97

hearted," Joan had said to him once. "How did she ever end up with the two of us?"

"But didn't you?" Helen was saying. "Didn't you like her?"

"Yes, I did. I mean I do. Still."

"If only I'd had a child," she said, "I could have given it to her like in a fairy tale."

Robert started to say something about the life such a child would have had, then thought better of it. Maybe if he didn't answer they could avoid the subject all together. The days of "trying" were long over, but the desperate feel of them still lingered. The thermometers and calendars, the shots he had to give, the forced march of appointments, and most vividly the unpleasantness of racing through the city in a taxi, a vial of his own sperm in a paper bag on his lap.

Joan had gone through all this too, of course, in the years when she was still married to that humorless French-Canadian. She and Helen were the only two in their set who were childless, and when the other wives talked endlessly of babies they would retreat to the porch and smoke in silence. Sometimes Robert wondered if they would have become friends at all if they hadn't shared this particular unluckiness. It was hard to imagine them being drawn together any other way. Helen with her sunny, forgiving nature, Joan with that dark thread of grievance that seemed to run beneath everything she said. Once, at a party, as she'd watched two of the wives tying cherry stems with their tongues, Joan had turned to Robert and said, "This is not the life I was intended for."

That aggrieved air had been there the first time they'd met too. Joan had sat next to them at a lecture they were attending on a rainy night, complaining about the vulgarity of someone who'd bumped into her with an oversized golf umbrella. She was a friend of a friend, Helen realized, and introduced herself. They were nearly neighbors too, they discovered, and so they made small talk about acquaintances and the neighborhood until the lights flickered. The lecture was on infertility, billed as the latest science, breakthroughs, that sort of thing. Robert had attended with extreme reluctance, but it had come to the point where he would do anything Helen asked of him in this respect as long as it kept her from crying. The speaker was introduced and Robert braced himself for a long droning talk, but the man was disturbingly lively with an alarming habit of clapping his hands to punctuate the points he was making. A few minutes into the talk, Robert realized that the speaker was, in fact, the only other man in the room. Women, women, everywhere, he thought, and not a drop to drink. Just then the leader singled out two women in the front row (one fat and sweat-panted, the other sad-eyed and lovely) and called them up to the stage. Their job, he explained, was to dramatize the struggles they had faced while trying to conceive. To this end, he designated the fat woman as the sought-after baby, the pretty one as the hopeful mother to be. From the audience, he recruited a small army of other women to stand be-hind the mother and pull and tear at her clothes, doing all they could to prevent her from reaching the baby. The play began and the women wailed and screamed and tore at the poor woman's clothes like cursed souls in some Greek myth. Others in the audience called out things and then more and more people jumped on the stage to serve as thwarters or cheerleaders. Before long, both women and most of the audience were weeping. Robert couldn't bear to look at Helen. He didn't want to know if her eyes were red. Silently, he plotted how to get them out of there, then suddenly realized Helen was standing. It was Joan who was holding out her coat for her. She already had one arm in. "Good Lord," Joan was saying. "What fresh hell is this?"

<«» «» «»>

In June, another doctor began looking after Helen. He was younger and his mouth twitched slightly, disconcertingly, whenever he spoke in the future tense. They had a new doctor because the old doctor had re-tired in May. It struck Robert as unprofessional, almost criminal, to leave a terminal patient like Helen. He wanted to file a complaint with some-one, with some board of review maybe, but Helen wanted no part of it. "Someone's always terminal, aren't they?" she said. "He can't just wait around until everyone's finished."

Joan was there when the new doctor reviewed Helen's charts and concluded that the old doctor's prognosis had been too optimistic. It could be weeks, not months, he said. They should at least be prepared for that possibility. Or it was possible that she could surprise them all and live much longer. "Who knows what will happen?" he said, his mouth twitching.

After the doctor left, Helen told them a joke.

Doctor: I'm afraid I have bad news.
Patient: What is it?
Doctor: You're dying.
Patient: Oh, God, how long do I have?
Doctor: 10.
Patient: Months? Weeks? Days?
Doctor: 9, 8, 7, 6...

《》 《》 《》

Summer then. She surprised them all by getting worse and worse but not dying. There was a month-long heat wave and then two straight weeks of rain. Helen watched the weather channel and fretted about her garden. About the weeds, about the deer, about the vegetables grown monstrous. Robert put off going there as long as he could, but finally one blindingly beautiful morning he drove over with a basket Sarah had given him.

He'd planned to go through the house first, take a quick look around, but when he tried his old key it didn't fit. He stood there for a moment looking at the door, then walked around to the gate beside the geraniums.

The latch made a satisfying little click when he let himself in. It was strange to be in his yard again. The sight of his old rake propped up against the shed made his throat close a little. The grass was high. The bushes needed pruning. Otherwise, it looked the same. He remembered all the parties they had had there, the way he used to string up lights in the trees. The garden was a mess, though not as bad as he'd expected. He watered it, then pulled up some radishes and zucchini, marveling at the size of them. After a while, it occurred to him that he should have gotten that pad Helen used to kneel on. Already, his knees were aching. A dim memory of church came to him. The sounds of bells, a silver plate. *Who made the world? God made the world.* The sun was higher now. It beat down on him. He wondered if he'd get a sunburn on the top of his head. There was a bald spot there now, the size of a quarter. He had only just noticed it, but it was hard to see and it bothered him to think of how long the spot might have been there. He stopped weeding and wiped his face with his shirt. An old, tattered one, but still his favorite. "Evolution Made Me Do It!" it said on the front. He thought of how he used to wear it to faculty parties. How all of the

The Tunnel

men had laughed and none of the women did. Once he'd passed Joan in the hallway while he was wearing the shirt and he'd seen from the sharp way her eyes flickered over him that she'd noted it. The last postcard she'd sent him had had a different tone. Cribbed from somewhere, he suspected. *You think you want the blue skies, the open road, but really you want the tunnel, you want to know how the story ends.*

By mid-day, his hands were hurting and his neck was red. There was more zucchini than anyone would ever want to eat. For once, the deer hadn't destroyed everything. Usually, they knocked a hole in the fence, but this year Helen had twined her fine blonde hair all along it. They hate the smell of it, she'd said, and it had pained him to think of her collecting it in the shower, practical until the very end.

«» «» «»

There was no Indian summer that year. September came in a flurry of storms. When he made it to the hospital in the driving rain, Robert felt exhausted as if he had performed some heroic task. What he liked best on these long gray days was to sit next to Helen and grade papers while she slept. He felt very close to her then, as if they had made it to old age after all and were winding down together in silence. If she woke up, she would watch T.V. companionably with him. Always the weather channel now. She wouldn't watch the news anymore or even those nature documentaries she'd once been devoted to (Lots of patients get this way near the end, the doctor had said. It's well documented, this particular obsession). There was one meteorologist in particular that Helen was taken with. The sad weatherman, she called him, because he always seemed so heartbroken when disastrous weather passed them by. Helen swore that once, as he was downgrading a hurricane to a tropical depression, the man had had tears in his eyes.

«» «» «»

Joan brought Helen the first fall apples, cutting them into tiny slivers so that she could eat them. When Robert came to visit, he would find the remnants of them turning brown in a bowl beside the bed. It was a source of great annoyance to him that everyone seemed compelled to make the same joke about them. *An apple a day...* said the nurse, the resident, the medical technician. "It's not working," Helen said.

It was not long after that that things started getting mixed up in Robert's head. Sometimes when he knocked on Helen's door, he felt an

Jenny Offill   101

odd excitement as he waited for her to answer. He felt young again, shot through with anticipation, as if he was going to see a girl he wanted, one he hadn't managed to seduce yet. But then always came the bleak correction of her body on the bed.

«» «» «»

"What do you talk about?" Sarah had asked him once. "Do you tell her all your deep, dark secrets?"

"No," he'd said. "Nothing like that."

"What do you talk about then?"

The weather, he told her, but she didn't believe him.

«» «» «»

There was, as it happened, one small secret he was keeping from Helen. The secret was that he'd taken her house key. He'd gotten it out of her purse one night when she'd fallen asleep and he'd kept the key in his pocket for a long time without using it. Mostly, it was enough just to feel it there, the cool metal promise of it. But one afternoon in late September, when the smell of burning leaves was in the air, he found himself turning onto his old street, then into his old driveway.

The house was as he'd left it. Nothing special, their old brick colonial, but still Helen had loved it. Perfect, she'd called the house that first day. He supposed Sarah would have laughed at that. She would have laughed too at the names Helen used for the rooms; this is the master bathroom, she would say, this is the parlor, this is the great room. But Sarah had never been inside the house. At least, there was that. He took out the key and let himself in.

Inside, it was cool and quiet. Robert admired the gleam of the wooden floors they had paid a fortune to have sanded just before he left. They had dithered for a long time over the stain and had ended up with something called dark honey, he remembered. He took off his shoes and slid across the floor in his sock feet. Something he had done as a boy in Brooklyn. He came to a stop in front of the mail table. Someone had been taking it in apparently. It was stacked neatly on the side table in a pile, but he didn't bother to look through it. What useful piece of news could there possibly be?

He went into the kitchen and found peanut butter in the well-stocked pantry. There was half a loaf of bread in the bread box. He made himself a sandwich and ate it, looking out over the yard. It was almost dusk, and he could hear the neighborhood children calling to one another in the street. Red light! Green light! Red light! Green light! Wasps had built a hive under the roof of the shed, he noticed. He took out his notebook and made a note of it. *Wasps?* it said. It occurred to him that he should fill the birdhouse with seed. Also that he should tighten the spigot on the hose. He took another bite of his sandwich, then stopped, something soft and furry on his tongue. I have eaten a mouse, he thought. How have I eaten a mouse? But when he turned over the sandwich, he saw that blue mold had bloomed in the corners of it.

«» «» «»

"I want to go home," Helen said. "I've had enough of this place." It was two weeks before Halloween. Robert thought of how it had always been her favorite holiday, of the parties they used to have in which all their friends came outlandishly disguised. "Dead Marilyn", Joan had been one year. A blonde wig and sleeping pills glued to the front of her dress.

No one tried to talk Helen out of going home. "We can make you comfortable," the doctor said. "There are marvelous drugs these days."

"Marvelous," Robert echoed and the doctor flinched slightly.

"We'll need the paperwork," Joan told him.

"Well then, best of luck," the doctor said, holding out a hand, then a nurse came in with the information for them. Among the papers was a list of hospice nurses. Joan asked for a copy of it and gave the original to him.

Robert had planned to call the nurses when he got home, but that night there was some unpleasantness with Sarah and he went to bed early, exhausted. That was on Wednesday. The next day, the hospital called to say they would be releasing Helen first thing in the morning. It was all much faster than he'd expected, and he had a class scheduled for the appointed pick up time. In a panic, he tried to cancel it, but Helen told him not to bother. Joan would drive her.

By the time he arrived at the house the next day, Joan had already interviewed four nurses and hired one, a small Filipino woman with a long melodic name and a silver cross around her neck.

"Catholic," Joan told him as soon as they were out of earshot. "Catholics make the best nurses because they take everything dead seriously."

"I know," Robert said. "I grew up with them."

She gave him an odd look. "Oh?" she said. "I didn't realize." She turned away then and began showing him the equipment that had been delivered. An adjustable bed, a weird soft toilet cover, some sort of monitor, and what looked like a morphine drip. The nurse was called back in to explain the proper use of all this, but later he realized he hadn't heard a word of it.

《》 《》 《》

It was decided that Joan would stay at the house now on the week-ends. The nurse was off then. It was decided that she would stay, but Robert had no part in the decision. Rather, it was announced to him one Friday when he was leaving. He was furious and went into the bathroom to get away from them, but the sight of Helen's old blue toothbrush nearly did him in. Next to it was a bright white one, clearly new. He stood there for a long time, staring at it, then he took it out of the holder and dipped it in the toilet. Later, after he'd put it back where it had been, he washed his hands with the tiny rose-shaped soap someone had provided.

《》 《》 《》

The day before Halloween, Helen got it into her head that they should all dress up in costumes. "I could be the skeleton," she told them, but no one laughed. Robert was dispatched to the attic to get the trunk, but when he brought it down and they looked through it nothing seemed right, and after a while even Helen gave up on the idea. "Let me hand out candy, at least," she said, but when the time came she slept right through it.

It was Joan who stood at the door and greeted the trick-or-treaters. Almost no one came and at the end of the night, there were buckets and buckets of candy left. On the drive home, Robert chewed taffy until his jaws ached.

《》 《》 《》

There was a breathlessness to the weeks that followed, a sense of jumping off into space. Helen was so clearly faltering that no one wanted to leave her even when the nurse was there. Everyone stayed all the time, knocking uncomfortably around the house together. One night, too exhausted to drive home, Robert fell asleep on the couch with his shoes on. In the morning, he was surprised to find someone had taken them off and covered him with a blanket.

«» «» «»

Helen died a few weeks after Halloween. She died on a night the sad weatherman had predicted flooding, but there was only rain. It was Joan who closed her eyes and pulled the sheet up to her chin. She hadn't wanted to wake him, she explained. It all happened so quickly. By the time Robert got up, she had dried her tears, called the coroner, and made coffee for them. Her voice when she told him was soft. Lightly, she touched his wrist. She put cream and sugar in his coffee and he drank it greedily, thankful for the sturdy fact of it. After he finished, Joan took his cup and washed it in the sink.

"Go home," she said. "You can't stay here."

«» «» «»

In the days that followed, Robert learned that he had been wrong about the will. There was another, newer one, signed while she was in the hospital. There were no vineyards or grand pianos or silver service, but in it Joan was named executor and in it, Helen asked to be cremated. Joan made all the arrangements within the week and when the box with the ashes came back, she drove to the cemetery and claimed it.

Of course, Robert knew he should have fought her on all of this, disputed the new will, gone to court even, but somehow it already seemed too late for that. He didn't even tell Joan what Helen had said to him all those years ago in one of those conversations lovers have in which everything must be accounted for, even death.

But sometimes, when he had no reason to, he would take a detour and drive by Joan's house at night. Sometimes the windows were dark. Other times, the blue glow of the television. Once he saw her washing dishes. Another time folding a blanket. He never saw her carrying the box of ashes and yet each time he slowed down on her street it was this that he imagined, that she would be sitting at the kitchen table, holding them.

On those nights that he spied on her, he went home feeling flushed, his heart too fast in his chest. Sarah could sense something, he knew, some transgression. She would not stoop to asking him where he'd been, or if he'd been with someone, she was not the sort of woman who did that, but she would turn a cold eye on him and say she was going to bed early, that she wanted to read for a bit. On those nights, he would remember the plans he'd once made with her, the great arrogant sweep of them. The world is waiting, he used to say. The world is waiting.

«» «» «»

Many years later, when Robert felt the twinge of dread that would signal his first and last heart attack, he turned off the lawnmower and saw once again the red curtains that had framed Joan's kitchen window. It was late afternoon. All around him the smell of freshly cut grass. Sarah at the picnic table, cleaning her glasses. Helen, somewhere. In the distance, a dog barked. Light bristled through the trees. A feeling like a hand pressing down on him. You! he thought. You! ●

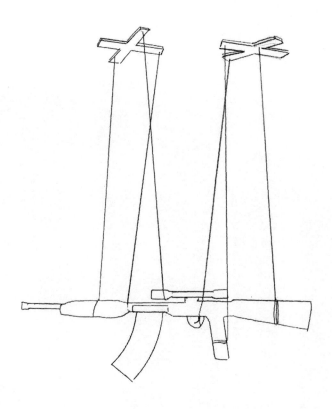

CONTR

Aimee Bender is the author of three books, and her fourth is forthcoming this summer. Her short fiction has been published in *Granta*, *GQ*, *Tin House*, *The Paris Review*, *Harper's*, and more, as well as heard on "This American Life" and "Selected Shorts". She lives in Los Angeles.

Adam Cvijanovic is an artist who lives and works in NYC. He can be contacted at adamcvijan@gmail.com

Patrick deWitt was born in British Columbia, Canada, in 1975. His debut novel, *Ablutions: Notes for a Novel*, was published in 2009 by Houghton Mifflin Harcourt in the US and Granta Books in the UK. Visit him at patrickdewitt.net

Rick Moody is the author of four novels, three collections of stories, and a memoir, *The Black Veil*. His new novel, *The Four Fingers of Death*, will be published in July 2010. He also plays music in The Wingdale Community Singers, whose new album, *Spirit Duplicator*, is out now.

Jenny Offill is the author of the novel *Last Things*, which was a *New York Times* Notable Book and a finalist for the *L.A. Times'* Art Seidenbaum Award for First Fiction. Her short stories and essays have appeared in *Story*, *Epoch*, *The Gettysburg Review*, *Boulevard*, and *The San Francisco Review of Books*, among other places.

A native of Long Island, New York, **Matt Sumell** is currently living in Los Angeles and finishing up his first collection of interconnected short stories, tentatively titled *Making Nice*. A graduate of UC Irvine's MFA program, he has been the recipient of the Arlene Cheng Fellowship in Creative Writing, the Glenn Schaeffer Award, and a Wagner Fellowship. His short fiction has appeared in *Faultline, The Brooklyn Review, Book Glutton, SaltGrass, The Greenbelt Review*, and *Noon*.

Adam Thompson's drawing installations and slideshows have been exhibited at various New York venues, including Thomas Jaeckel Gallery, Crossing Art, and Dixon Place. He is an art reviewer for *Art Papers* magazine, and his writing has also appeared in *The Brooklyn Rail, Art Notes*, and *Flavorpill*. He produced the art for *Bicycle* by Paul Fattarusso (Hotel St. George Press, 2008). Adam received his BA in Art History from Yale University (2004) and his MFA in Visual Art from Brooklyn College (2008), where he now teaches art. A book of his drawings is forthcoming in May from Regency Arts Press. He lives in Brooklyn with his wife, writer Helen Phillips.

BOOKS

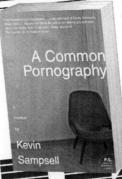

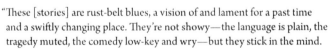
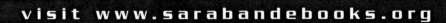

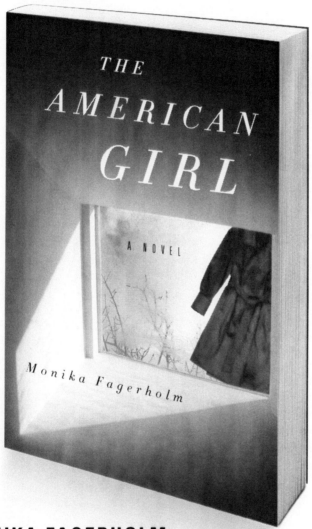

SUBSCRIBE TO ELECTRIC LITERATURE!

Electric Literature is an anthology series of contemporary fiction. We select stories with a strong voice that capture our readers and lead them somewhere exciting, unexpected, and meaningful. And we publish everywhere, every way: paperback, Kindle, iPhone, and eBook.

Please use the form below to subscribe by mail, or go to electricliterature.com and subscribe online.

1) What's your name?
....

2) What issue would you like to begin your subscription with?

❒ Issue 1
Michael Cunningham, Jim Shepard, T Cooper, Diana Wagman, Lydia Millet

❒ Issue 2
Colson Whitehead, Lydia Davis, Marisa Silver, Stephen O'Connor, Pasha Malla

❒ Issue 3
Rick Moody, Aimee Bender, Patrick deWitt, Jenny Offill, Matt Sumell

3) How would you like to receive Electric Literature?

PAPERBACK
❒ Within the USA and CANADA ($48)   ❒ International ($90)
shipping address:
....
....
email address:
....

ELECTRONIC ($24)
choose a format: ❒ PDF ❒ ePub ❒ LRF ❒ Mobi
email address:
....

A subscription to Electric Literature is 6 issues.
Please make all checks payable to Electric Literature LLC

Send this form, or just write the information down on a piece of paper, and send it with a check to:
Electric Literature Subscriptions, 325 Gold St, Suite 303, Brooklyn, NY 11201

Lightning Source UK Ltd.
Milton Keynes UK
UKOW05f2106241013

219757UK00001B/369/P